I0543681

Drops from the Kingdom

Copyright © 2009 Larry Itejere

Published 2011

Cover Illustration © 2010 by Stephen Beckstrand
Layout and Design by Larry Itejere
Official website: www.larryitejere.com
FB: www.facebook.com/dropsfromthekingdom
Manufactured in the United States of America

ISBN: 978-0983882909

Library of Congress Control Number: 2011914076

Acknowledgement

*****

Every fire as you know begins with a spark. That spark for me began with a statement from my sister in-law Lacey. "Why don't you put it on paper..." she said. If it wasn't for her you wouldn't have the first book from the Drops from the Kingdom series.

I would also like to thank my wife and kids for their support. To my in-laws Lacey and Dawn Martin thanks for your suggestions and review. To my friend Stephen Beckstrand who helped me in creating the cover and map, thank you.

I would also like to thank everyone that has helped in making this book a success. I hope you enjoy it as much as I have in bringing the story of the people from the four kingdoms to you.

TABLE OF CONTENTS

PROLOGUE... 9

CHAPTER 1 15

DREAMS SEVENTEEN YEARS AGO 15

CHAPTER 2 28

THE VISITOR FROM BREMAH 28

CHAPTER 3 39

THE ANAMERIAN UNLOCKED 39

CHAPTER 4 48

THE GREEN BOX 48

CHAPTER 5 69

BOUND BY THE OATH.................................. 69

CHAPTER 6 79

THE WAY TO BAYSHIA.................................. 79

CHAPTER 7 86

UNEXPLAINED CONNECTION 86

CHAPTER 8 99

LADIES OF THE DEEP 99

CHAPTER 9 110

THE RISING SHADOW 110

CHAPTER 10 121

A MESSENGER'S VISION 121

CHAPTER 11 136

WHY THEY PONDER.................................... 136

CHAPTER 12 144

THE PRINTS OF THE UNKNOWN................... 144

CHAPTER 13 156

A TOWN IN CHAOS.................................... 156

CHAPTER 14 171

UNDELIVERED MESSAGE........................... 171

CHAPTER 15 182

GONE IN FLAMES 182

CHAPTER 16 195

BEGINNINGS TO DISCOVERY 195

CHAPTER 17 210

A WELCOMED SURPRISE........................... 210

CHAPTER 18 222

THE MIST TO LUFGARD 222

CHAPTER 19 233

NEW REVELATION 233

CHAPTER 20 240

MEMORIES AND LETTING GO 240

CHAPTER 21 252

A HOLE TO THE ABYSS.............................. 252

CHAPTER 22 263

HISTORY BEHIND THE STORY 263

CHAPTER 23 272

THE AWAKENING 272

CHAPTER 24 282

THE SPARK OF HOPE 282

CHAPTER 25 287

KEEPER OF THE GATE 287

CHAPTER 26 295

DEAD END 295

CHAPTER 27 305

HOPE REKINDLED 305
CHAPTER 28 314
COURSE OF ACTION 314
CHAPTER 29 325
STAIN OF DEATH 325
EPILOGUE 339

Prologue

The sound of soldiers and their horses could be heard around camp as tents were set up for the night. Nearly eight thousand men moved about, carrying out their varying tasks as lights from the campfires lit the area. In the midst of the sea of people, a man in his thirties which was close to his middle years, stepped out of his tent and into the cold winter's night. Resting on the man's chest was an amulet that he tucked underneath his garment the jewel of the one endowed with the power of an Anamerian. Outside, the steady snowflakes that had fallen during their journey had stopped, leaving a white blanket over the area. With a quick glance at his surroundings, the Anamerian made his way to the back of his tent, staying close to the edge. He stopped a quarter of the way to the back, poured out the contents in his cup, and then shook his hand in a whipping motion, clearing out the remaining drops. Satisfied that the cup was clean enough, he made his way back to the front of his tent. On opposite sides of his entrance, two guards were sitting on the ground with their legs crossed, unperturbed by the chilly night, even though one could see that their clothing provided no protection from the cold.

These guards were Ackalans, which means "Guardians," and no ordinary men. The Anamerian lifted his tent flap and walked inside, aware that the Ackalans were watching, even though no heads were raised. They sat there like statues, unruffled by the wind or cold.

Inside the Anamerian's tent was a small, ornate table that stood two feet from the ground. On top of the table was an ink jar with a feathered pen. Beside the jar was an open scroll of paper with a small clay oil lamp next to it.

The glow from the oil lamp lit the area around the table that showed signs of use. The Anamerian walked over to the cushion behind the table and sat down, crossing his legs. As he leaned forward, the light from the oil lamp illuminated his face. His eyes were amber, and his cheekbones were well-defined behind his trimmed beard and mustache. Lost in his thoughts, the Anamerian lifted the feathered pen and began to write, as visions of the events that led him and the men he was now leading reopened in his mind.

"How did we get here in such a short time?" he wondered. "Our people have changed because of this war that leaves those who survive in bondage, and in only seventeen years."

The words seemed to strike a nerve and he paused, trying to stop his hand from shaking as the amulet underneath his shirt lit up and the oil lamp on his table suddenly began to flutter.

He took in several deep breaths to dowse his anger as a sense of determination slowly overcame what was once a personal guilt. As the tension in his body began to abate, the light of the oil lamp stopped wavering. The Anamerian released his grip on his pen, placing it back on the table. He rested his head on his palm and moved his finger back and forth across his forehead, staring at the paper in front of him; his expression was deliberative, as if deciding whether or not to continue writing. Time passed before he reached out and picked up his pen again.

"The land and its people have changed," he wrote as his hand moved across the page, "because of the one referred to as Gaid'dum, which means Death's Soul. Some believe he has all of the keys of creation, which would make him immortal, and so cannot be killed or bound by men. Some say, at his command, he could move the Earth itself, while others claim that he is a god.

"While rumors of his power continue to spread across the land, there are those of us who know the truth about him.

"Records from archives reveal that a boy, whose name was Sullivan, touched what no man was allowed.

"Immediately, the power within the scroll claimed his body without him knowing. It began twisting his mind, leaving him with a single desire: the uncontrollable urge to find and acquire the power of creation from the other keys that were spread across the land. While no one knew how he did it. Sullivan was somehow able to obtain most of them; and as his power grew, so did his influence on mankind. Creatures from the abyss once regarded as myth began to appear, serving his purpose as they slowly destroyed the land.

"Thousands have lost their lives in our fight for freedom, which now hangs at the verge of annihilation with the memories of the once-glorious days of the empire fading with the dead like long-forgotten dreams.

"Our enemies appear out of balls of fire and disappear with the wind. They destroy everything in their path, sweeping across this land like an avalanche; taking homes, mothers, fathers, children, and their livestock.

"They kill everything without regard, and all that remains at the aftermath are mutilated bodies. Then there are the markings, charred, concave ring formations that appear on the ground the only sign of their presence.

"In most cities and towns destroyed by these creatures, their great walls and gates provided no security, as they were not touched; but inside were the same charred concave rings with the dead strewn everywhere. While death and suffering loom over the land like the headsman's ax, we find hope in the three that lead our cause. Though never been seen by most of the people in this company, the rumors of their ability and strength have spread across the land, as far as Gariban, north of Ditra-Vashine to the land south past Eura. They alone stand as a beacon of hope for all. Why these three were chosen to be responsible for the fate of so many, including mine, I do not know, but I believe it is no coincidence they lead our fight today; were it not for them, our cause would be futile.

"Over the years, we've found representatives and rulers from what remains of the four Kingdoms which are represented by the prominent cities of Bremah, Ditra-Vashine, Eura, and Bayshia, building our army with the hope of a new dawn and the day when we shall take off the head of the serpent."

Chapter 1

Dreams Seventeen Years Ago

Sunlight crept into Iseac's room, slowly reaching out till it brushed over his face, pulling the twelve-year-old away from the place he would have liked to stay another minute. It was that dream–the one he started having when he turned nine. In his dream, he always found himself at the entrance of a cave in an area that was densely forested.

The entryway into the cave was triangular in shape, with three deep cuts on top that looked like claws. Moss and vines covered most of the area surrounding the entrance, making it appear ominous, but Iseac was not afraid.

He'd also come to notice that there was a stillness to the place. It lacked the natural sounds you would expect in the middle of the woods. The trees around him stood in silence, allowing little beams of light to shine through tiny gaps between their branches; so he knew it was still daylight.

Iseac walked into the dark cave, which slowly narrowed the farther in he went. Drawn by something he could not explain, and with each step he took, his feet made a soft creaking sound, like slipping stones. This sound quickly faded, until he could only hear himself breathing against the sound of his footsteps. After several minutes of walking in pitch blackness, the narrow entrance opened up into a wider area. A section of the cave was lit by bright yellow stalactites that ran into areas he could not see. The roof had touches of shimmering blue streaks that ran along their spiky tips. Several feet from his position, he could see a gold wreath, which rested next to three clay balls sitting atop a boulder. The boulder stood about four feet from the ground, with the top flat, and its body was cylindrical in shape, as if man—made. It had similar blue streaks on the roof running down its side.

Iseac walked over to the balls and could see cracks in them revealing a glowing, silver-like ore.

He placed the wreath on his head; it seemed to fit perfectly. When he broke open each clay shell, he found three shiny statues in the form of young men. Two of the statues had something in their hands, one a bow and the other a sword. The third held nothing; its hands were missing.

He found himself entranced by their magnificence as he brushed his hands over them. They were smooth as an eggshell and strong as a crystal, and what he found fascinating about the silver-like objects was that they were not cool to the touch, as one would expect of the metal. Whenever he began to study them, he woke up.

Though sporadic, the dream was exactly the same, except for one thing. The expressions on the statues were different; it was as if they had a life of their own, with their form changing slightly every time.

Unaware, Iseac began developing a strong kinship to the statues, a link or connection of sort, which he could not explain. Whenever he woke from one of this dreams, he stayed in bed, hoping to make it return, but never able to. He tried figuring out if a particular thing or pattern triggered the dream, determining over time, that it had nothing to do with his food, mood, drink, or even the weather. He needed to find a way to trigger it on his own, as the urges to remain in the cave continue to grow with each episode.

The sun was over the horizon when Iseac woke up from the dream. It had been three weeks since his last one and it weighed on his mind as he got ready and left with his father for their farm.

Out in the field, Iseac had no idea his father was watching him throughout the morning as they worked.

"Iseac!" his father beckoned, gesturing for him to come over. It was the middle of the day now. Iseac stopped what he was doing and began making his way over to his father, unaware of how little he'd accomplished in clearing the weeds around the still-germinating crops.

Is it already noon? Iseac thought as he made his way. It was the indicator they were halfway through for the day.

Lenard sat under the tree at the center of the

farm, away from the sun, as Iseac approached.

"You seem distracted, son; is everything all right?" he asked as Iseac sat down.

"Yes, I'm fine."

"I have seen you working before, you know; is there something wrong?" Lenard asked more pointedly as Iseac shook his head.

"Then what's the matter?" Lenard asked.

Was it that obvious, Iseac thought as he moved closer to his father, who was handing him some bread, cheese, and smoked meat that they'd packed.

Iseac was quiet for a minute, looking out into the field with the sun blazing overhead; that was when he noticed for the first time how little he'd done in clearing the weeds.

Normally he would have covered twice the area in the length of time they'd been working. He knew he couldn't shrug off his father's question and that he was waiting for an explanation.

"Something I can't really explain happened again to me last night."

Lenard gave him a quizzical look, the one that

said, 'Do you really want me to ask?' so Iseac proceeded to tell him about his dream and why it was troubling him.

Lenard listened intently as he ate and drank from a leather pouch containing water that he had buried in the ground to keep cool while they were working.

When Iseac was done narrating the events of his dream and how he felt after each episode, Lenard brushed the crumbs off his fingers and sighed with his last bite disappearing. After a few seconds of pondering what Iseac had told him, which was more than most fathers would have done for a twelve-year-old, he said thoughtfully, "Have you heard the story of the Ackalan, or Kalans of the Silver Scroll, as they are now known, son?"

"Yes," Iseac replied, wondering why or how it related to his dream.

Lenard gave Iseac a knowing look. His head tilted slightly with brows raised, urging him to explain.

"I heard they were a chosen group of men

given charge to protect some silver scroll of creation," Iseac said.

"More than that," Lenard replied, as he told Iseac the story of the man who was chosen to be the first watcher of the scrolls of creation and how his dream led to the discovery of the po'ra fruit that ran through the veins of every true Ackalan today.

Iseac looked at his father, trying to draw some correlation to his issue as his father continued to speak. "Dreams are life's truth. They tell of one's desires, fears, and fantasies. They sometimes even give glimpses into our future. The key to your dreams is finding out what the three statues represent. The fact that they are made of a silver-like material could mean that your fate might be tied to theirs, but that is only if your reflection appears on the statues, I was once told. Does it?" Lenard asked curiously.

"Yes!" Iseac replied excited.

"That might explain why you don't want to wake up. Now, since I'm no dream interpreter, I think you should talk to someone that might be able to make more sense of it.

"Hmm," Lenard said, pausing for a minute, obviously thinking. "I believe Tamican might."

Who is this Tamican? Iseac wondered as his father continued to mumble to himself.

"There is someone who might be able to help," Lenard finally said. "In two days, a merchant crew is going to be in town. I want you to tell this person everything you told me."

Lenard then stood up. "But right now, we need to get back to work. Come on," he said as he walked back into the field.

As he said, a merchant's crew came to Tru'tia two days later. The person they were meeting on this day was at the Oak-Ore Valley Inn. After speaking briefly with the innkeeper, Lenard led them up the stairs to the last room on the second floor.

He knocked on the door and an audible voice from inside the room answered, "Come in."

It was a female voice, which for some reason Iseac was not expecting.

"Wait here," he told Iseac just before pulling

the oak door open. "I will be back soon." With those words, he stepped in, closing the door behind him.

A few minutes later, Lenard stuck his head out the corner of the door as Iseac stood waiting at the entrance. He invited him in.

Inside, Iseac couldn't help noticing how odd the setup was. There were two archways, each wide enough to admit one adult at a time.

His father was barefoot, with his shoes neatly set to the side.

Lenard motioned for Iseac to do the same and remove his shoes. Once Iseac was done, he pointed.

"Go through that archway, I'll meet you inside." He watched Iseac make his way through the right entryway.

Iseac did what he was told and made his way through the right archway. He could smell incense made of scented flowers. The archway curved in, and he could see his father looking in his direction waiting. Both entrances converged like a horseshoe.

There was a brief introduction as Iseac stared at the strange setting.

A petite woman almost in her middle years sat on a cushion inside a dome-shaped room. Brightly colored fabric of yellow, gold, red, green, and white ran along the wall of the dome to the cushion around her. Her dress, like the wall, was of bright colors, with her skirt spread over her legs.

She said, looking at Iseac, "Your father tells me you've been having the same dream sporadically for some time now. You want to know why and what it means?"

It was almost three years now, Iseac realized, since he started having this dream.

"Yes," he said with reverence.

Her voice was clear and carried the wisdom of someone who knew many things.

"Do you know that different sounds and colors mean something in a dream?" she asked.

"Take the red belly Chamar, for example. If this bird is sipping water on a leaf, it means it's going to rain before the end of the day or before midday of the following day," she said and went on to give other examples, making sure Iseac understood that every detail in one's dream is important.

"Now tell me about this dream of yours and in as much detail as you can remember."

Iseac cleared his throat and began to speak, telling her everything he could remember. It wasn't hard, since everything was still so vivid in his mind, and even with that, Tamican still asked more probing questions on little details Iseac had chosen to ignore.

Iseac could not help noticing her sense of surprise. Whether it was good or bad, he wasn't sure. When Tamican was done, having been focused on Iseac the whole time, she turned to Lenard.

In her eyes, Iseac could see her putting the pieces of information she'd gathered from him together as silence once again filled the room. After a minute of watching her move her head up and down several times as if coming to a conclusion, she said, looking at Lenard, "Your son is truly special." Then she turned to Iseac.

"While your dream has many facets, it's all about you and your destiny. I will tell you everything I can, but I need to talk to your father alone for a minute."

Iseac left the room a little disheartened; what was so important that she needed to speak first with his father alone? Nothing in her demeanor or tone indicated there was a problem, so why they were making him leave made no sense. After all, it was his dream and she did say it was about him.

After Iseac waited for what seemed like hours to a young boy his age, all the while wondering what they could be talking about, his father stepped out the archway.

"Get your shoes on," he said, and he began putting on his own. "I need to speak with your mother." Lenard had the uncertain look of someone trying to make sense of what he had just been told.

"So what did she say?" was Iseac's first thought, but he did not say it or try to press his father on what they talked about and why she couldn't answer his questions now. He got his shoes on and they left the room.

Iseac knew it wasn't terrible news since his

father wasn't biting the corner of his lip. His father did this subconsciously when he had distressing news.

"Tamican would like you to meet with someone else when she returns in a week," Lenard said, and he could see the disappointment on Iseac's face, his expression giving away his feelings about the news.

"Son," he said, speaking solemnly, "your dream is no ordinary dream, as you must have figured out by now. The answers will come, but we all need to be ready."

This did not console Iseac, but caused an even greater anxiety as different thoughts ran through his head. It was going to be the longest wait of his life.

Chapter 2

The Visitor From Bremah

Unlike most other days, Iseac woke up early
without the normal prompt from his father. The
day he'd been waiting for had finally arrived. He
walked over to the corner of his room and took out
the last polished stone from the jar he was using to
count down the days leading up to Tamican's
return. The anticipation filled his appetite, driving
away his usual desire for food.

"I'm not hungry this morning," he told his
mother as she offered him breakfast.

"Are you okay, dear?" she asked.

"I'm fine," Iseac replied.

"You need your strength if you are going to get
any work done with your father. Now come, sit
and eat something, son."

Iseac saw no point in arguing, so he sat down
and began nibbling on his food when his father
walked into the house. Passing the kitchen table,
he said, "Remember we're going to see Tamican

today, so take an extra shirt."

The rest of that morning was a blur for Iseac, as his thoughts were consumed by Tamican's visit and the stranger she was supposed to be bringing with her.

At noon, as directed by his father, Iseac changed to a clean shirt and they made their way to the inn where Tamican was staying.

"You can tell me all about your visit with this person Tamican will be introducing you to when you return."

"What?" Iseac replied, looking at his father. "Do you mean you are not coming with me?"

"No, not this time," Lenard replied, remembering Tamican's words; *He would like to meet him alone.*

"Why?" Iseac asked.

"I believe the person coming with Tamican wants to meet you, and not us."

Iseac did not like the idea that his father wasn't going to be there.

"You will be fine," Lenard said, seeing the concerned look on his face, "and besides, you will be in capable hands."

They made their way into the inn and up the stairs to the room where Tamican was supposed to be staying. As they approached the landing, they saw her stepping away from her door. She greeted them on the landing and asked Iseac, "Are you ready?"

"Yes," he replied with the subtle eagerness of a boy as they made their way downstairs.

A few people sat at the bar, with some serving girls wiping off tables as they exited the inn.

Outside, Iseac stood beside his father, who patted him on the shoulder.

"I will see you at home," he said to Iseac before nodding his head toward Tamican to excuse himself.

"Walk with me," Tamican said, drawing Iseac's attention away from his father leaving. She appeared to be dressed in less flamboyant colors than last time, but her dark purple and red slit gown still seemed bright under the gray sky that was a stark contrast.

The grounds were muddy from rain the night

before. As they walked, they passed several familiar shops with few people on the street. They turned right into a narrow alleyway between two buildings and continued walking. They made their way past several more shops with their names mounted on wooden plaques above. Though it was past midday, the clouds still held.

Iseac could see passersby on the other side of the street between sections of buildings parallel to theirs. Tamican stopped in front of what was once a wood shop.

She followed the side of the building and stopped close to the back, where there was a smaller building that appeared almost as an extension of the main shop in front.

The door at the entrance was flush with the side of the shop, and if it wasn't for the landing in front, no one would notice. Just as Tamican stepped on the platform, someone inside the house spoke.

"Come in," a male voice said before she had a chance to knock.

Amazed, Iseac looked at Tamican, who did not

seem the least bit surprised.

"We hadn't made any real noise on our approach, so how did the man inside know we were at his entrance?" Iseac wondered as she opened the door and stepped in. He followed closely behind her.

Iseac wasn't sure what to expect, especially after his last meeting with Tamican. Hopefully this time someone would finally explain to him the meaning of his dream. He took in a deep breath to slow his racing heart; he had waited a long time for this moment.

Inside, the house was warm from the fire burning at the hearth. A rug was spread out in the center of the living room, with three oak chairs at the edges of the rug.

On the right side of the room was a bookshelf with a hanging map to the left of it. The place looked like it hadn't been used in a while. Some of the fixtures had a notable amount of dust on them, and the smell in the room was that of a place not long swept.

The man who stood in front of him was

slightly older than his father—not as tall, with his head shaven. He wore a deep green cloak intricately designed in the front. Iseac could tell from the pattern that it formed a symbol if pulled together. His trousers were dark brown, tucked inside his black riding boots. His tunic was light blue and it extended halfway to his knees; this was supported at his waist by a brown belt.

The man gave Iseac a warm smile as he introduced himself, calling him by name. "Peace and prosperity, Iseac. I'm Gabram." He bowed his head slightly.

Looking up at Tamican, he greeted her with the familiarity of an old friend, and she responded in the same manner.

"Please have a seat," he said to Iseac, gesturing to a chair by the hearth. As Iseac did, Gabram began to speak with Tamican. They moved toward the entrance door, but something caught Iseac's eyes. The ring on the man's finger—he'd seen it somewhere before, but where, he wondered. And then it struck him. The lightning on the ring: he was a Patron. His father had told him stories of meeting a Patron and about their rings, and now he was in the same room with one.

From what he was told, Patrons were always present at the inauguration of a king or queen, and that it had been that way since the creation of the four Kingdoms.

Outside of that, he knew nothing else about them.

Iseac could not make out what they were saying at the level in which they were speaking.

"I hope we meet again soon," Tamican exclaimed, catching Iseac's eye.

"I will see that he gets home safely when we are done," the man said, seeing Tamican to the door.

Iseac rubbed his hands on his thighs while trying to maintain his impassive look, but the anticipation of finally getting an answer filled him as Gabram walked back.

He pulled one of the chairs by the fireplace and sat a few feet away, directly in front of Iseac.

He then proceeded to ask Iseac questions about himself and his family, which Iseac wasn't expecting, thinking he was going to go right into the matter of his visit and not waste any time getting to know him.

Iseac answered each question, still in disbelief that a Patron had traveled all this way for him, a twelve-year-old boy, to explain his dream.

"I know you have been waiting for some time now to find out about your dream and that you feel a particular connection to the one you told Tamican," Gabram said. "That is the reason I'm here, to tell you what you are..." Gabram began to explain to Iseac what his dream meant.

This was not what Iseac was expecting, but then, he wasn't sure what he was supposed to expect. The words his father had said the first time they had left Tamican—"We all need to be ready"—played in his head.

Looking back, he could see why Gabram was trying to ease his way into what he was about to tell him, knowing that it would change his life forever.

"Terrowin was the youngest Anamerio we had on record, called at age fifteen, until today," he

said. "You are the second I now have had the privilege of meeting. Do you know what Anamerio means?"

Iseac shook his head in response.

"It means soul finder or seeker. An Anamerio or Anamerian is a person born with the rare ability to see or tell key events before they happen, serving as a counterpoint in restoring or bringing balance to all things. Only one lives in every dispensation, and this is due to their rare trait called *The Falling*. A gold wreath is always present in their more significant dreams, like yours. As an Anamerian gets close to the end, the leaves on the wreath start to fall. This continues for the rest of his life until he passes. When this happens, the wreath is passed on to their successor, who sees it in his dream right after, and that is why it is called The Falling."

Gabram could see shock and disbelief on Iseac's face as he listened, trying to process what he was being told.

"You have a special gift, Iseac, and I have come to help you develop it," Gabram said.

"It's just a dream and can't mean this," Iseac

thought, trying to convince himself that it could not mean what he was being told, but he knew inside that wasn't true. He knew he was connected to the dream, but it did not explain why he was chosen.

"Nothing is special about my family, so why me?"

"I do not know," Gabram replied honestly as he studied Iseac, seeing him slowly accepting the news.

"What happened to the last Anamerian?"

"He passed away three years ago," Gabram said.

Iseac remembered that was when it started happening.

"I need to make preparations and would like to meet your parents. Can you take me to them?" Gabram asked.

Iseac nodded in response, still bemused. He could see that Gabram seemed convinced he was the Anamerian; he did not think he was.

After their meeting, Gabram walked back with Iseac to his home, where he met his father and mother. Iseac's mother tried to maintain her composure as she offered Gabram a drink before returning to Lenard's side. Around the Patron, his parents showed a feeling of awe that Iseac had never seen, but who wouldn't? Outside of royalty, very few people could say they'd had a Patron in their home.

Iseac was excused so Gabram could speak with his father and mother alone, but this time he had an idea of what they were going to be talking about—this special person he was supposed to be. He was called in about an hour later and asked to see Gabram off.

Outside, Gabram told Iseac that with his parent's permission, he would meet with him every fortnight for the whole day.

"I am Kayma to you; it means guide," Gabram said, "and you will address me as such whenever we meet until I tell you otherwise. Have a good night and I will see you soon." He walked away into the night.

Chapter 3

The Anamerian Unlocked

As arranged, Iseac met with Gabram at the house behind the old wood shop every fortnight. "Having a perfect understanding," Gabram said on his first day, "is the key to bringing balance in anything." He handed Iseac a map, instructing him to study it. This was how he began his first day of education and training. Throughout Iseac's first year, Gabram never explained the reasons for the task he was assigned until the end of the day when he was tested, which made things sometimes frustrating. It was mainly academic at first, learning about the different cultures and land across the Kingdom. He also learned about different weaponry, their strengths and weaknesses. He left home for the first time just past his fourteenth birthday to study the history of the Anamerians and also to develop his innate ability in the use of the quarterstaff by a master of this weapon.

It was hard leaving home for the first time,

especially for his mother, even though she knew he was only going to be gone for several months. Their life as a result of his gift was changing faster than most parents could be prepared for.

He remembered the emotional good-bye with his mother standing at the door of their home, waving as he rode off with his father to meet Gabram close to the border of Tru'tia.

"We've always been proud of you, son," Lenard said as they stood by their carriage. Those words seem to break Iseac, who had been trying to be strong. He was sniffling as his father pulled him into an embrace. He brushed Iseac's hair once and then released him.

"We will see you soon," Lenard said, watching as Iseac made his way to Gabram, who was waiting. He was gone for a year.

It all changed from that point, and for the next several years as his training intensified. The time he could spend at home became less. This was particularly hard on his relationship with Elena, a girl from his hometown, whom he was suppose to be betrothed to.

At eighteen, Iseac was prepared for his first test. He stood in the center of a sandy arena surrounded by blocks of wood six feet tall. The blocks were paired in sections of four, with a three foot gap between them. A platform slightly higher with a bench was built next to the arena and there Gabram and his Quartermaster, Darum, sat, watching.

The morning air was cold, but the anticipation of what was about to begin kept Iseac warm. The rule was simple: he had to make sure he wasn't hit three times in the next three hours or it was all over. Very few people ever made it to a master, and this was his chance.

There was no warning sign from both men watching him as it began. He had to fight and defend himself for three relentless hours. The attacks came from all corners as men dressed in sandy green camouflage rushed into the arena with their blunt weapons. Sometimes two attacked him at once, other times, he had four. Iseac stayed focused on the people entering the area, ignoring those who were running around on the outside, trying to confuse and distract him.

The first hour went by quickly and by the second hour, he was beginning to feel the strain from the constant motion with his quarterstaff. When the third hour rolled in, he was covered in sweat. He had two strikes within a short period as he lost track of time from fatigue. He knew there was no way he could stave off the six people who were rushing toward him, so with his last strength, he leaped over their heads. He was struck by a long-spear as he landed.

"Enough," the quartermaster commanded on his third strike and everyone in the arena stopped. It was all over.

Iseac dropped on one knee, holding onto his quarterstaff, disappointed that he lost. Gabram and his Quartermaster, Darum, walked into the arena.

"Well done," Darum said, standing next to Iseac with his hands clasped behind him.

"I can't believe I failed," he thought, not completely listening to Darum.

"You made it, Quartermaster Iseac," Duram said with a level of pride in his tone. "I will see you inside."

It took a second for those words to sink in even as Gabram came over to congratulate him. Iseac could not believe it; he had made it.

"You held them off longer that most other masters, except yours, Duram, of course. Over four hours is very impressive," Gabram said, tapping Iseac on his shoulder.

At age nineteen, Iseac was finally prepared to meet the Patrons of the eight temples. He had learned over the years about the Patrons and the organization that remained a mystery to most people, even after hundreds of years. The Patrons were keepers of the secrets of their world and the true nature of man.

They were gathered at the Grand Hall, where he was summoned. Iseac remembered feeling eyes following him as he walked up the hallowed room with the Patrons sitting in a circle, the Chief Patron at their head.

The Patrons sat on a flat, cone-shaped stool of pure marble that rose three feet from the floor. The tiles on the floor were designed in the pattern of a star with eight points, each end pointing to a seat. The Patrons each seemed to reflect the lights hanging from the walls that appeared to separate them as they sat with their legs crossed.

Gabram had made sure Iseac met each of the Patrons during his training, and Iseac recognized each of them as he made his way to the middle of their circle.

He recognized Buldric with his black curl, who was the Patron of Mevi-tra, also known as the land of rocks because of its landscape. Muras, with green eyes like seaweed, was the Patron to Wing-high, which was located east of Bayshia. Erasmus, with slant eyes, was the Patron of Tollan, north of Tru'tia, a land surrounded by bamboo trees. Casimir, with his broad shoulders, was the Patron of Seer-Root, built around a swampland in the midlands. Adal, with his dark skin, was the Patron of BanSun, located in the sandy plain known as the home of the sun. Cyriac, the oldest of them all, was the Patron of Air-light, located on the eastern region of Ditra-Vashine, with the Kadan River to the east.

Gabram, with his shaven head, was the Patron of Rod Stone, where they were now gathered on Mount Va'lenna; Thorlak, with his white beard, was the chief Patron and head of Amera-line, located on the icy plain in the north. Each man had the symbols of his keys engraved on his ring as presiding Patrons of the various temples.

Lips did not move, but Iseac could hear the chief Patron Thorlak speaking. His voice was soon joined by another and then another until they all joined as one, forming a single voice. The day had finally come, and he took in a deep breath to clear his thoughts as he stood in the middle of them.

A single pulse like a wave ran through his body from the tip of his toes to the top of his head, sending a surge of energy that slowly overcame him until he felt caught in a whirlwind. The walls around his mind slowly began breaking. Images outside his surroundings flashed in and out of his mind as wave upon waves of unknown memories rushed through him. The surge converged in his head, and he felt lost in the world that was opening up to him.

While this was going on in his head, the amulet on his chest, given to him by Gabram, came to life. The thread of golden lines at the center of the amulet moved in and out of each other, unlacing themselves until they revealed a fuchsia-colored crystal—the amulet of the Messenger.

Once the amulet was lit, the Patrons slowly released their focus from Iseac, and the pressure that seemed concentrated on his mind began to abate. The once-dormant parts of his mind lit up like a kindling stick and began to burn bright even as he continued regaining his strength. When Iseac opened his eyes again, he knew the history of each Patron, his lineage, and the history of the land. The room they were in was a hub; it allowed each Patron to access the power of the respective scrolls.

The air seemed different; colors of energy ran through his mind's eye as if they were alive. He ignored them, focusing on getting his strength back. Even as this was happening, the memories of the Anamerians before him continued to merge with his own.

He remembered the settlers before the

establishment of the four Kingdoms, which was over a thousand years ago, like his other memories. Years of learning about the land and history of the four Kingdoms paled in comparison to what he now knew, giving him a complete understanding of the world. He knew where everything was—roads, trails long abandoned or now covered in trees, secret tunnels, lakes, and springs. He was a living master map.

Thorlak spoke to Iseac with his lips still motionless, "A shadow of change is brewing, the likes of which mankind has never before witnessed or seen. We need to be ready. The three you seek are running against time. With your true self revealed, Sullivan will be looking for you to get to them. You need to bring them to us before he finds them or you. Remember, the beacon of the three will burn brighter when you are close. So listen when you are prompted to act."

And this was how it began: Iseac, understanding that he needed to search the world for three people he'd never met before, using a gift he did not yet understand.

Chapter 4

The Green Box

Gabram continued to work with Iseac after his unlocking into their last weeks together. The speed at which Iseac recalled information, even from over five hundred years ago, was getting increasingly faster. His bond to the Anamerians before him was strong.

Gabram tested Iseac's ability in controlling the air, which he did by drawing on the knowledge of Alizarin. The forth Anamerian before him born in the desert plain.

Changing tactics, Gabram began questioning Iseac on different situations and how he would use his knowledge to protect himself and those he would be leading with the least amount of casualties.

Iseac's responses to Gabram's questions at first weren't quick as his mind raced through libraries of information, knowledge drawn from the Anamerians before him. His thoughts filtered through their life experiences like childhood memories, and with each following question, his answer came faster.

Iseac, with each passing day, was gaining a greater understanding and awareness of the world around him, but there was also something else going on with him that he could not explain. At first he ignored it as a fluke until it happened again: natural light changed into a reflective mass for a brief second and then returned to normal.

Iseac assumed it was part of the change that comes with one's unlocking and wasn't expecting a reaction from Gabram when he mentioned it in passing.

"Really?" Gabram said, his curiosity piqued. "What..."

"What you just said a second ago, that sometimes the light seems like a reflective pool. I was wondering when you were going to say something about it. I was beginning to wonder if you had it."

"What do you mean, have what?" Iseac asked.

Iseac saw the look he had come to recognize

well in Gabram when he was about to show him
something most people would consider impossible.

"All Anamerians inherit this gift; however,
their ability to use it varies depending on the
individual. Did you see images inside and around
the Grand Hall during the unlocking?"

"Yes," Iseac replied, wondering why.

"Yosterio," Gabram said with some excitement.

"Yoste. What?" Iseac asked, knowing he would
explain.

"Yosterio," Gabram corrected. "That is what it
is called in the old tongue. It means 'mirror
boarding'; it is a special gift that allows you to see
things outside your surrounding by setting an
image in your core."

Iseac looked at him, lost. "I'm not sure what
you mean."

"I'll show you," Gabram said, seeing clearly
that Iseac had no idea what he was talking about.
"Get on one knee and close your eyes. I want you
to think of something you saw outside today,
something close to the house. Signal when you can
visualize it in your mind."

Iseac did when he was ready.

"Good; now place the image in your core," Gabram said. "Place the tip of your finger on the floor and let the image in your core flow through it."

As Iseac did, he felt a sudden sensation like a ripple run from his body into the ground. A wall of fog appeared in front of him and within his mind's eye; he flowed through it and could see the exact yellow flower outside and other plants around the house. Shocked by the experience, he opened his eyes, breaking his concentration and connection to his core.

The expression on Iseac's face was enough for Gabram to know that he had done it. Iseac looked up at Gabram, his eyes wide with surprise.

"That was yosterio," Gabram said with a smile. "If you can hold your concentration long enough, you can see beyond your surroundings. While other people go to sleep hoping they are safe, you should always go to bed knowing you are. Always check your surroundings as far as your mind will let you."

Even though Iseac's first experience of yosterio was strange, frightening, and exciting at the same time, he quickly picked it up. It was like riding a horse after eighteen years: you never really forget. The process was exhausting, especially the farther out he reached his mind, and he quickly learned that there was a limit to stretching one's mind. Once he had to stay in bed for two days to recover his balance after holding on too long.

They returned to Rod Stone temple on Iseac's last day in preparation for what would be the quest of his life. When he got to his room, there was a long case on his bed.

It was slim, about five feet long, and next to it was a note that read:

"Now that you are ready, I believe this may come in handy." Nothing else identified the person who left it, but he had his suspicions.

Iseac opened the case to find an amazingly well-crafted quarterstaff. It was polished deep brown and, at a casual glance, looked almost black. The middle was wrapped in woven leather about six inches wide. Both ends were wrapped in metal rods that were the same color as the wood.

Lifting it up, Iseac was impressed at how perfectly balanced it felt in his hands.

After supper, Iseac decided to go down to the temple archives, which were below the main floor. He made his way down several flights of stairs made of marble tiles that curved down, leading into a short hallway. At the end of the hallway stood an oak door with metal inlays that extended into the wall as part of the design. The door itself had no visible handle, just a small metal panel. The massive room was filled with ancient records and vast numbers of books. Iseac was hoping to find something interesting to get his mind off the big announcement that was happening the next day. He perused several of the scrolls, books, and maps, and after several hours, decided to head back to his room. As he rose to leave, something caught his eyes—a little green cylindrical box knitted in a finely crafted pattern. It felt out of place beside the other books. Iseac pulled out the box and opened it to reveal a scroll that looked untouched. Curious, he broke the seal and began to read as the words came to life in his mind.

****

Alicia, the midwife, and her maid ran in and out of the bedroom preparing warm cloths, sheets, and ointment as Archena groaned with pain; the day had finally arrived that she would be delivered.

"The cerinum roots will ease the pain; just chew," Alicia said to the laboring mother as her maid moved over to her back, making sure she was propped up enough by shifting the pillows behind Archena's back for more support. The maid returned to her side, wiping off the beaded sweat that spotted Archena's brow using a damp rag.

"Now take slower breaths," Alicia said as she checked on her progress. "You are doing just fine."

Alicia's presence had a soothing and reassuring feeling. She spoke calmly, with the confidence of someone who had done this a thousand times.

The raining season was over and so, like every other day during this time of the year, the sky was clear blue with no clouds in sight. The sun was almost at its zenith, with the air hot and dry, when something strange happened. The sky started to change in the middle of the day.

This was not the natural gray sky that came with cloud cover; instead, the sun was losing its light and being overshadowed by darkness. Those on the street turned to look at the heavens. Within minutes, the sun was gone and it was pitch-black, like midnight. Widespread panic rolled through the streets as people ran to their homes for safety.

Silence filled the void as the streets became empty, and while nothing stirred, a faint sound suddenly broke the silence. The almost cat-like cry was coming from the herbalist shop, something that a few minutes ago would have been lost in the noise outside. It was the unique and unmistakable sound of a crying child, and a short time later, Archena was handed a little boy wrapped in white swaddling. She rocked her crying babe gently only the way a mother can.

The pains from her experience were an almost—distant memory as she smiled at him, her face filled with the joy of a new mother. The rocking motion of her back and forth soon sent the babe to sleep, and she too drifted off to sleep a few minutes later, drawn in by exhaustion.

While mother and child rested, three women walked briskly along a narrow pathway behind several homes with orange glowing windows that came from the light inside. It was a footpath of compact clay that joined the main street, which was empty. They moved with a single objective, ignoring the sound of everything around them, their intent as clear as their destination.

A creaking sound came from the door opening at the herbalist shop, followed by several footsteps as someone walked in. Alicia had been busy putting away some of her remedies held in little wooden containers on the lower shelves at the front of her shop and was hidden by the counter in front.

It wasn't strange or surprising to have a visitor in the middle of the night when there was a problem that couldn't wait until the next day. So it was a little surprising to find three members of the village Council standing at her doorway and looking around.

Dressed in their usual brown gowns with wide

hanging sleeves, the inside of the dress red, they looked at her. The hoods of their cloaks were held down together above their chest by a crystal broach that rested in the middle of their bosom. The crystal gleamed as it reflected off the lamplight inside.

Each woman had a different color broach denoting her position. The crystals were either white, which was the lowest rank, then brown, red, or black, which was the highest rank or position within the Council. In these parts, members of the Council were revered as spiritual leaders and judges. However, they rarely meddled in civil affairs, even though they had that right.

"We seek the names of all mothers that were delivered here today," the woman with the red broach said as she stepped forward. She was short and stocky with her hair pulled back, revealing her round face. The two behind her also stepped forward so that they were less than an arm's length from her. Her tone was direct, leaving no room for question.

"Of course," Alicia said without hesitating.

She leaned to her side, stretching her hand underneath her counter to grab a note, which she placed on the counter. Once they had the information they came for, she curtsied and they turned and left without saying another word. Alicia stood there for a minute, marveled by what just happened. She knew with Council business you do what you are told to honor your house, and that meant everything.

The following morning, Alicia checked on Archena and the babe, making sure they were fit for travel.

"Take two spoonfuls of this for seven days," Alicia said, handing Archena a small jar. She then gave her some advice on feeding, cleaning, and generally taking care of her babe.

She wrapped a cloth that hung loosely just below Archena's bust, with both ends of the cloth tied in a knot over her left shoulder, creating a cradle. She placed the child in the makeshift carrier in the front, and when they were ready, Alicia saw her to the door.

Dew was still on the trees in the cool morning

air when Archena left with her son. It was going to be another hot day, with the sun already lighting the sky with its presence.

Archena was beaming like every new mother as she walked home. She was looking forward to showing her new pride and joy to her family, relatives, and the people in the surrounding area of her village.

She knew, though, that parading her son would mean listening to the unwelcomed advice of every mother who knew this was her first. "No matter," she thought, still in awe of the child she carried in front of her. The roads had the normal stream of people this early in the morning as she walked, checking on her son regularly. Passersby occasionally exchanged greetings, and as it got warmer in the day, most people walked by the side of the dirt road, using the trees for shade as the sun licked the remaining moisture from the ground, leaving the red dirt road flaky.

By midday she was on the stretch of road that led to her village, and from her vantage she could make out the position of her house. It was a modest home, built on a platform that stood a foot from the ground, made from clay mixed with straw. It was light brown outside and gray on the inside, so it was cooler during the dry season, which was the hottest time of the year. Most homes had a garden, which separated the houses, but Archena's had trees that stood high above her straw-roofed home.

As she drew closer to her house, the back of the building now in sight, there was no welcoming party, which was strange. It was customary that family and close friends checked frequently for the arrival of the new mother. The child is introduced by the father to the family and given a name.

Music and celebration normally followed the brief ceremony. The women would have people watching for her arrival. She started wondering what could have happened to everyone. Observing her surroundings more closely for sign of disturbance or trouble, nothing stood out, but it did not feel right. Something obviously had happened while she was gone.

As she turned the corner, the entrance to her

home now visible, she suddenly felt her heart drop.

Members of the Council stood at her doorway next to her husband, Hammond. "What would members of the Council want with us? Are they waiting for me?" She thought, hoping her fear was unfounded.

"What is going on?" she asked, trying to to sound worried as she met Hammond halfway. He looked heartbroken, even with his attempt to smile.

His eyes were dim, not the look one would expect from a proud father. He tried not to look at the child, fighting the longing. Clearing his throat, he spoke before Archena could ask another question. "Let's go inside," he said, leading the way, the Council following behind.

"No, I'm fine," Archena said lightheartedly. "I've only been gone for two days. I know I can still serve and find my way around this house. If I need a drink, I'll get one."

It was expected as courtesy to offer a guest seat and a drink, since Hammond made no such offer to their guest before she sat down. She knew they had been waiting for her, which made what they had to say more unnerving.

"Now, come, sit," Archena said, gesturing to Hammond. "We don't want to keep our guests waiting."

A Council member stepped forward once Hammond sat down. She was above average height and past her middle years, with streaks of gray in her hair. She spoke in an almost declaratory tone.

"We, the Council, have come to claim all children marked by Rami-hado, translated to mean 'hand of the shadow', whose spirit was stretched over the sun, turning it to blackness. The child you hold was marked by his birth. He must be cleansed as it is written."

The words struck Archena's heart like a blacksmith's hammer and for a second, she could not breathe.

In her mind, she cast the words away, not believing what she just heard. Her world was about to fall apart. "No! It cannot be...he is our first," she said, her voice quivering as she spoke, while trying to maintain some composure. Like a cracked dam at the brink of eruption, she held her emotion.

It was expected of delta women that any outward expressions of emotion only happen in the solitude of their home. Archena was in shock. There was nothing she could say or do that would change things now. Once the Council had spoken, it was final.

"Angela will take and ready the child," the Council member said. "The washer is waiting for you at the back; the water is ready so we can begin your cleansing so Rami-hado might not possess your seed." Her tone was flat and empty of any sympathy.

"Please come with us," Hilda said as Angela took her son away. It was heartwrenching letting go, like losing a part of herself. The baby started crying.

Supported by Hammond, she was led to the back of their home. A small tent made from banana leaves had been erected. Twenty feet from the house, steam oozed between the layers of leaves as she walked over to the woman who stood waiting. Removing all her clothes, she walked into the makeshift tent.

The heat inside was intense at first, but slowly her body adjusted. Inside the middle of the tent was a vase filled with boiling water containing herbs, buried in a hole, supported by hot coals, with another pile on the side. Archena could hear a single drumbeat...tap, tap...that slowly changed into a succession of rhythmic beats. The people outside chanted while keeping up with the beat as they moved around the tent; it had begun. Alone, she let her tears flow freely.

In her solitude, she wondered if she would ever see her son again. It had been over a hundred years since something like this had ever happened in this village. Thinking about it, she realized that the children who were taken never returned...

"But it will be different this time," she said, interjecting her own thoughts. It will be different this time.

After several minutes that seemed like an eternity, the drumbeat stopped. The makeshift door to the tent was pulled open and she was beckoned. A woman stood at the entrance with a green sheet for her to cover up as she stepped out. Her face, shoulders, and arms were glossy with sweat as she was led back to her home.

Once inside, she noticed her son was already dressed in red swaddling. She was no longer allowed to touch him. As Angela and the baby headed for the door, an audible voice that couldn't hide its aching spoke. "Stop!" They all turned to look at Archena. She asked if they could wait for a minute and ran into her room. A second later, she came out with a necklace that held an emerald ring. She placed it on the babe, careful not to let any part of her touch him.

"This is his," she said, placing on him her most precious possession, a family heirloom. Angela looked at Hilda, making sure it was okay. She nodded slightly to give her approval, and they left.

As the Council journeyed into the forest, they had two other babies with them, a boy and girl from two other villages. It was a half-day's walk to the Shrine of Olinar buried inside a cave. As they journeyed into the forest, Angela could not help but wonder about the baby she was holding. When he was crying and she touched his hand, a tingling feeling ran though her body and his eyes flashed from brown to silver, but she said nothing about it.

The sun was setting when they arrived at the entrance of Olinar's cave. Two Council guards stood at the entrance with a spear in one hand and a raised shield on the other, so it was over their chest. Others hid behind trees that served as camouflage. As Hilda led the group into the cave, a male voice spoke from behind them. It was loud and clear.

"Stop!"

Everyone that heard it, did, and they turned in the direction of the command. Hilda, who was now behind the group, made her way to the front. And while her face held no expression, she was going to show the person who dared stop them the sharp side of her tongue.

Once in front, she could see six armed men in circular formation, weapons in hand. They were covered in cloaks made of animal hide and tree leaves that allowed them to blend into their surroundings.

They were the priestess guard, the highest-ranking member of their Council. The guards were tall men with faces hidden behind brass masks, their bodies wrapped by their cloaks. They watched their surroundings like hawks, with eyes searching for anything out of the ordinary.

The guards in front parted, revealing a woman in her older years. Her hair was pure silver gray, which was a contrast to her smooth skin. She wore a white-laced dress that was illuminated by the green and gray around her. Hilda and her company bowed their heads as she walked past them.

"Rise, child," she said to Angela, whose head was bowed. She rose with the babe that had the emerald necklace around his neck. The priestess gently loosed the cloth wrapped around the child and her eyes widened. She stared at his hands and then began to speak almost prophetically.

"He cannot enter Olinar. He is of the lineage of Lamtin and shall bring freedom to us all, but blood and destruction will set his path. Soon people will have to choose, and many will follow him to their end. Two stand with him, and our fates are tied to theirs, but only he has access to all the keys..."

****

Iseac could not believe what he'd found, an account of one of the three. Reviewing the document again, it prophesied of some great battle to come. It said nothing about where the child was taken, other than the fact that he was never returned to his family. He rolled the scroll and placed it back on the shelf. His biggest concern had been where to start, and this document had just made it clear. He would begin his search heading west toward the island now called Rehaj.

Chapter 5

Bound by the Oath

The sun was still behind the horizon, even though signs of dawn marked the heavens, when three men stepped out of the Rod Stone temple, their distinct light-blue robes catching the firelight as they made their way toward the courtyard where men known as Ackalans, or Kalans of the Scroll, were gathered.

The Ashra, or commander, of this group of Ackalans was a man named Tremay. He had his eyes fixed on the temple doors, watching as the men known as Patrons approached. When they were in a close enough proximity to hear him speak, he announced in a loud voice so those in his company could hear. "We have come to heed the call and fulfill our oath. *Ta-respir a'new mania*," he chanted, meaning, "For our honor and duty to the oath."

The Ackalans gathered in the courtyard joined Tremay, repeating in unison "*a'new mania*," "to the oath."

The chief Patron, Thorlak, walked over to the podium, which was a small wooden stand. He raised his hands in the air to acknowledge their salute, which was ritualistic.

"So are we, to the truth that binds us all," he said before

putting his hands down, and it was once again quiet.

Thorlak looked out into the group of men gathered and began to speak. His voice rose and fell with the strength of an old man who was wise as all eyes were fixed on him.

Two men stood on opposite sides of Thorlak as he spoke. Like him, they were dressed in their silk Patron's robes, which were light blue. Torches were posted on columns around the yard, and the firelight seemed to reflect off the Patrons' robes, giving them a glow. The chief Patron's hair, mustache, and beard were white, and his eyes were brown.

Thorlak had a gold ring with a round blue stone on top, which pulsated with flashes of light, while the men that stood next to him had green stones. Their rings were the only item of distinction in their clothing.

"A war is coming, the likes of which mankind has never before seen," Thorlak said. "It will ravage the land and push mankind to its brink. The signs of its beginning are appearing around the four Kingdoms, but we shall overcome this force that threatens to rip apart the fabric of our society; for in the darkness, a new dawn will arise as we hold onto the flames of freedom.

"The Anamerian has returned with the amulet of the Messenger, which has once again been revealed," he said as he gestured toward Iseac, who, taking his cue, stepped out into the open. "Follow, protect, and fulfill your oaths," Thorlak said as the men turned to look at Iseac.

"We have received and we shall fulfill. We ride with the Messenger," Tremay said as Iseac came to stand next to the Patron. Thorlak gestured for Iseac to go as his horse was brought to him. The Ackalans waited for Iseac to mount his horse, then the men all got on their horses. Led by Tremay, they trotted out the temple gate, heading north, which led to the city called Bremah.

It was still midmorning when Iseac and the Ackalans made their way in a trot down the mountainside. Rod Stone temple's entrance rested on the northeast corner of Mount Va'lenna, with the front landing built in on a semi-circle, supported by four pillars that looked like a crown. Each pillar was inscribed with a symbol of the sun, wind, water, and earth. These massive pillars looked like they grew out of the mountainside, each balanced at the base by what was called the hand of time. The ledge from the top spiraled around the mountain.

As Iseac rode to the head of the group, he counted sixty-five men riding in his company. The men were all uniformed with their dark brown cloaks and black boots. The hilts of all their weapons were engraved with the symbol of an Ackalan, and outside of that, they had no visible armor.

The Ackalans were masters of most weapons, which

included the double-edged ax, sword, and spear. They had the ability to hear and see beyond normal sight. Their senses were heightened from mastering their body and surviving the po'ra, or fountain fruit, only found in Mevi-tra. This freezing tundra was said to be the area where the first seed of creation was planted.

The po'ra fruit had the ability to cleanse or kill those who ate it. For the Ackalans, it served as a reminder of their call and duty. The perilous fruit remained in their system, trying to kill them, while they mastered its flow, moving it to their subconscious. The cleansing power of the fruit caused a silver ring to appear around their pupil, which was more pronounced at night. This awareness allowed them to be alert, even in their sleep.

The nearest town, Bremah, was a day's ride.

"Ashra...my goal is to make it to Bremah before nightfall," Iseac said as he rode next to Tremay. "Please inform your men, then join me."

Tremay turned his horse around and trotted back to his men; when he returned, they picked up their pace, intent upon reaching Bremah as soon as possible.

They galloped and trotted across creeks, miles of meadows, and long spans of forested areas with narrow and wide trails. The sun rose and was beginning to fall when the Red City came into view just over the horizon. Tremay raised his hand to the square, slowing everyone behind him to a canter.

Bremah was called the Red City because the streets were made of red cobblestone, and even some of the homes were built with the same reddish stone. The wall around the city was about five stories high and extended as far as the eye could see. The area around the city wall was an open meadow, making it hard for intruding forces to come upon the city without being spotted from miles. It was ruled by Queen Viasen.

The land, though, had changed since the last time Iseac remembered being in Bremah. He wondered for a second if it was his own memories or those of his predecessors, both slowly becoming indistinguishable.

The smaller villages and farm towns farther away from the city were now abandoned. He could remember not that long ago when the villages were growing, and he couldn't help but wonder why they were now abandoned. The people they rode past seemed more cautious.

Farmers herded their animals alongside the packed earth that made up the road to the city. There were people on mule carts, or pulling handcarts, and less than a handful were on wagons heading along the long stretch of road into the city. Guards could be seen on towers around the city wall and at the eastern gate where they were heading. A light flickered in the distance, and Tremay knew they were being watched.

People moved out of their way as they approached the entrance into the city.

Two armed men, dressed in scaled sheets of iron breastplate with the insignia of the crown on their left breast, stepped out in front of them, bringing everyone to a halt. They knew who the Ackalans were, but this was protocol. The man to the right of Tremay spoke.

"Welcome to Bremah, Ashra," he said in his Ma'hian accent. "It is required that a party greater than eight, as decreed by the Queen, be entered in the books. You must also declare your exit gate and return to it on your departure. How many are in your company?"

"Sixty-six," Tremay replied, "and we'll be leaving at the western gate."

"Will any portion of your company be staying when you leave?"

"No."

"Please wait here," the guard ordered.

As they stood waiting, the guard walked over to a man sitting in a booth at the corner of the gate. They spoke briefly, and the man in the booth started writing something down.

When the guard returned, he raised his hand in the air, signaling to the tower guards who were all watching with their bows drawn and waiting that all was well.

Everyone knew the tower guards were renowned marksmen that some said were Golans.

"You may enter," he said, moving out of the way. The guard returned to his post to resume his watch.

The sun was almost below the horizon as they trotted along the main street inside the city wall, passing merchant shops that were beginning to close for the day. Peddlers and hawkers alike were clearing the streets, as most people began preparing for the night.

They took their first left by the Wine-Hoppers Inn, heading west of the city. The part of the street they were on was noticeably older, just like the buildings themselves. They passed several other streets with shops already closed.

It wasn't long before the setting sun, that was grayish—orange, turned into complete darkness. Lights soon appeared in windows above some of the shops and they could see the silhouettes of people moving about in their homes. They followed an alleyway to a gate just wide enough to admit two mounted riders. Tremay stepped off his horse and tapped the gate three times. Someone slid open a peep hole to see who it was. He looked at them for a second and then slid it shut without saying a word.

They heard two short squeaking sounds of something

being disengaged just before the gate was pulled open and they rode in.

Inside the gate stood a single three-story building made of stone; it was cylindrical in shape, with an archway that led inside. In front of the structure was a long pole that held the banner of the Silver Scroll on top. The walls inside the gate had fire posts mounted around them. Led by Tremay, they rode in a procession as they made their way through the archway to the heart of the courtyard in the center of this cylindrical-shaped building.

Iseac couldn't help noticing how well designed their fortress was. As he looked up and around the building complex, he could see doors through the wooden balcony on the second and third floors.

They stopped at the center of the courtyard and their horses were taken to the stable at the back.

Tremay led Iseac to the second floor and stopped at the entrance to one of the rooms.

"I will bring you word on any information I gather tonight," he said before nodding to excuse himself.

As he turned to leave, Iseac called in a tone just high enough to get his attention. "Ashra!" he said, asTremay turned. "Meet me at dawn in my quarters."

Tremay nodded his head in acknowledgment of Iseac's

request. Iseac, in turn, nodded his head to excuse himself before walking into his apartment, closing the door behind him.

It was early in the morning with the sun still below the horizon when Tremay walked up to Iseac's door. "Come in," a voice audible enough to be heard outside called before Tremay could knock.

He stepped in and saw Iseac looking over what he suspected was a map. He gestured for Tremay to join him, which he did, walking over to stand by his side. He looked at what Iseac was staring at on the table. It was a map, just as he suspected.

"So, what information were you able to gather?" Iseac asked as they studied the map.

"There are rumors that everyone from one of the villages outside Bremah called Utorm disappeared about a week ago, and no one knows what happened to them," Tremay said.

"Some of the king's men were sent to the village to find out what happened; they found nothing but empty homes. From what I gather, they found tracks of a large number of people herded into the woods, and then their tracks ended abruptly, as if they all vanished. They questioned neighboring villages, and the only thing they found common amongst the townsfolk was a short period when their animals went wild."

Tremay paused for a second. "The word of a whole village disappearing has started spreading, and people in the neighboring villages are worried."

"Was there anything else?" Iseac asked.

Tremay shook his head.

"Hmm...it is beginning to spread," Iseac said, not explaining what he meant. "We will be heading to Erua..." Iseac said, pointing at a location on the map, "and then continue into Bayshia proper."

Iseac was already dressed for travel, with his quarterstaff leaning against his bed.

"Let your men know we leave at sunrise," Iseac said, turning to face Tremay.

"We will be ready," he replied. With his right hand on his chest, he bowed to excuse himself and walked out of the room.

When Tremay returned to Iseac's quarters, he was packed and ready to go. So they made their way down the stairs in front of the courtyard, where a stableman stood waiting for them with their horses. Once Iseac mounted Durack, his horse, they rode out of the courtyard toward the main gate that was pulled open as they approached. They turned left and headed for the western gate.

Chapter 6

The Way to Bayshia

In the land south, in a small town called Chartum-Valley, morning dew was still over the farm when Samuel woke up. The aroma of pork and fresh bread filled his nostrils as he rubbed his eyes and sat up by the edge of his bed. Looking around the room, the other two beds were empty.

Samuel hurriedly put on his trousers and wool shirt, pulling both laces to close the top half of his shirt. He found his boots by the side of his bed, slid his feet in, and tightened the laces.

"I can't believe they didn't wake me up, today of all days," he said as he rushed out the door, following the direction of the scent inside the house. He heard the low murmuring of conversation in the same direction he was heading.

"Come!" Harold said, when Samuel was in sight. "Sit down, boy. Your food is getting cold. I was going to send your brother to come get you. We need to get the bales and crops on the wagons before sunrise." Samuel walked around the table to an empty seat. He could see his father's bowl was already empty as he continued to listen.

"As you know, we have a long day ahead of us, and we

need to get your mother some supplies," Harold said as if it was just another day, even though he knew the harvest festival was in three days.

The harvest festival was the biggest celebration in the known Kingdoms, and it was being held in the city called Bayshia.

The ride to Bayshia was a three-day journey, and his boys were looking forward to it. They all knew this, and since he was the last one at the table, Samuel ate fast, trying to catch up.

"Slow down, boy, or you might just choke yourself," Harold said with a smile while shaking his head. "We aren't planning to leave without you, you know."

Samuel caught himself; his thoughts had been racing with all the things he was planning to do in the city, and he didn't realize how fast he was eating.

"I will pack some extra food for your journey," Celina said. Faray, her oldest son, and Elye, the youngest of the family, finished their food and hurriedly headed for the door. Their excitement was just as apparent; they were going to the city!

It wasn't long before Samuel joined Elye and Faray outside as they enthusiastically loaded the wagon, doing it faster than their normal pace. They each talked about what they were going to be seeing, buying, and doing in the city.

When Harold came out to join them, the wagon was already packed. "If only they were this fast on other days," Harold said to Celina as he kissed his wife by the front door entrance. He moved to the wagon and checked to make sure everything was secure and ready to go.

Samuel and Elye jumped in the back of the wagon, legs dangling as they rode toward the farm gate. Faray, who was the oldest, rode his brown bay next to Harold at the head of the wagon. They waved at their mother, who stood by the side of the house waving back as she watched the wagon roll out of their farm.

Chartum-Valley was a small farm town with two mills owned by Peter Lyman and Godfrey Cherie. Stan Martin ran the blacksmith's shop with his son, Owen.

They had three stops to make on their way to Bayshia, first in the town of Orie, which was a two-day ride, and then at three inns in the next town, where Harold did his trading before going to the city.

Whitney Gaynor's inn, the "Ladies Nest," was always their first stop. When they arrived, they stopped at the corner of the inn and Harold asked Samuel to join him.

They went through a side entrance into the building. As a boy, this was the first two-level building Samuel had ever seen. The inn was always clean, with plenty of food, drink, and music. Rich merchants and nobles only used Whitney Gaynor's inn when they were in this part of town, and it was rumored that Prince Paron had visited once.

As mistress of the inn, Gaynor was poised, with a face that was always welcoming, yet at the same time, one not to be trifled with.

"Welcome!" Betria, one of the waitresses, said, seeing Harold from a corner table. "I'll let the mistress know you are here," she said before darting away.

A few minutes later, Gaynor stepped out from behind the double door that led into the kitchen and other rooms at the back.

"It's good to see you, Harold," she said with a smile as she turned to look at Samuel, who was standing next to his father.

"He's turned into a handsome young man. I still remember your first visit to Orie as a little boy. How the years truly go by quickly."

"Yes," Harold said, agreeing with her sentiment.

"So, is he still fascinated with the bow and arrow?"

"Yes, he is. Ever since he could walk," Harold replied, "and he is impressively good, too."

Samuel felt embarrassed hearing them talk about him. He was now seventeen, but they talked about him as if he were still nine, even though he was proud to hear his father speak of him with such high regard. The topic changed to the rest of his family, and then to the purpose of their business.

"I'll have someone open the cellar so they can start unloading," Gaynor said.

Calling on one of her maids, she instructed her about what she needed done and promptly sent her away. She turned her attention back to Harold.

"If I may be excused," Samuel said, bowing his head toward Gaynor, "I will join Elye and Faray to unload the wagon." He made his way to the main entrance as the voices of Harold and Gaynor talking slowly faded behind him.

By the time Samuel joined them, they and Gaynor's male helpers were almost done unloading the part of the wagon that belonged to her.

Their next stop was Wayk Ritchie, a man just past his middle years with a little streak of white on his hair.

He always had a pipe at the side of his mouth. When he smiled, you could see the gap in his front teeth. Ritchie had come a long way since owning this tavern.

Where there had once been frequent, violent brawls, there were now only the occasional quarrels. Most wives came to his tavern when they were looking for their husbands, and he knew a lot about the affairs of those who Patronized his establishment.

It was dusk by the time they got to Silla Coal's inn. She was Harold's older sister—skinny and small, but she had more white streaks in her hair.

They unloaded the rest of the items on the wagon, and that evening had supper in the kitchen. Elye, Samuel, and Faray shared a room, where they spent the rest of the night playing a board game and talking about what they were going to do in the city of Bayshia.

Samuel was looking forward to trying again at the archery competition. He was not going to settle for second place this time, after barely losing by two points in one of the challenges. He'd spent a lot of time practicing when he wasn't working in the field.

Elye was looking forward to the magic show that always came into town at this time; there was always something new in every show, and he'd enjoyed the show since the first time he saw it with his father.

Faray was looking forward to seeing Klair, the daughter of a wine merchant named Aram. He and Harold were friends before they moved from Chartum-Valley to Bayshia, and Faray had known Klair since they were young. He hoped that one day she would be betrothed to him, if he ever mustered the courage to ask her out on a real date. "I'm going to do it this time," he thought to himself.

Faray seemed lost in his own thoughts when Elye said to Samuel, "Well, we know what he's thinking about...Klair!" he said in a teasing whisper.

"No, I'm not," Faray sneered.

"I don't know much about girls," Elye continued, "but I know that until you summon the courage to ask—"

"Yes, you don't know anything about girls," Faray cut in, "and the delicate act of courting." His tone had a slight agitation in it.

"Okay..." Elye said, dousing the little spark of irritation he seemed to have kindled. They went to bed some time later after finishing the game.

It was early morning the next day and the sound of roosters crowing could be heard at different parts of the town as Harold, Faray, Samuel, and Elye made their way out of town. A few people were in the street, sweeping around their shops, while others were getting ready to leave for their varying tasks.

The morning was hazy, with the sun still behind the horizon, as they rode out of Orie. Once the town was behind them, the horses picked up their pace. With the wagon empty, they rode faster toward Bayshia.

Chapter 7

Unexplained Connection

The city of Bayshia was fortified by an inner and outer wall. It was the first of its kind, built generations ago by an ingenious king. In an attack, it was said that the city could sustain itself and its people for years.

Bayshia was known for its industries and goods, which were popular around the four Kingdoms. The city seemed to draw master craftsmen of all kinds, including wood and stone, which was evident in some of the amazing structures inside the inner wall. But what set the city apart from the rest of the Kingdom was its advancement in weaponry, which King Portman sometimes showed off to his people so they knew they were safe.

Beyond the city were miles of open meadow, with rolling hills and trees at the horizon.

During the celebration of the harvest, which happened every three years, peasants were allowed to set up camp inside the outer wall of the city for a small fee.

The inns inside were filled with travelers from around the land, with merchants arriving days ahead of time, making the prices during this time outrageous.

As Harold, Faray, Samuel, and Elye rode in past the outer wall, Samuel thought there were fewer tents this time than the last time they were at the festival. It did not seem as crowded inside the outer wall. Maybe it was just him; besides, three years was a long time ago, and a lot had changed, including his own perspective now that he was older. As their wagon rolled along with the crowd into the inner wall, the sound on their approach steadily grew, like entering an arena filled with people. Visitors could not help but be consumed by the sense of jubilation.

Even though the inner wall was also crowded, it wasn't as bad as the last time Samuel remembered attending the festival—they had to push their way through the crowd. This didn't mean that it still wasn't crowded and loud as they celebrated the season. They just didn't have to push their way through as much this time.

Guards stood at every intersection, keeping watch as usual, and the shops were still packed with people. Street hawkers moved about, displaying their goods as they cried out to get people's attention. Along one of the streets were young girls and boys with painted faces and bright-colored costumes performing juggling acts and acrobatics, trying to draw the crowd to their show.

An assortment of conflicting musical instruments was

playing all around them, mixed in with the sound of the crowd itself; it was an exciting time. These outdoor shows were only allowed during the harvest celebration.

"Boys, be at Stone Hog before dusk," Harold said as Samuel and Elye jumped off the wagon, eager to explore.

"I will stay with Father to get Mother's provisions; good luck on the competition," Faray said to Samuel as they rode off, disappearing into the crowd.

Samuel and Elye made their way through the sea of people toward the eastern corner of the city, where merchants outside the city had their goods on display. The vast area had hundreds of booths, and it was claimed that during the harvest festival, you could find anything you were looking for, from clothes in their varying styles and fashion in the four Kingdoms to livestock that included exotic animals not found in these parts. Herbs that merchants claimed could cure any ailment, to ointment, tools, and endless kinds of jewelry.

The lively sound of chatter filled the air as they walked, viewing the different items on display. Samuel, who was a tall young man for his age, could see from their position the two-story tent with its rainbow of colors that was the site of the magic show five booths away.

"I don't understand what you find so interesting about magic shows at fourteen, but...they're your coins."

Elye did not respond to Samuel's rhetorical question; his excitement was still the same as the first time he saw the show.

"I'll join you once I'm signed up for the competition," Samuel said as Elye stood in the growing line and others joined him, waiting to get in.

"I won't wait for you if you are not on time," Elye said as Samuel turned left, disappearing between two tents. He made his way down several makeshift footpaths created to accommodate the traffic.

After several minutes, Samuel came to the familiar booth with the name "Ramthon Flight" carved on a painted plaque above.

Adam, a skinny man with a narrow face who was past his middle years, was watching the street when Samuel walked up.

"Ah...the young man that took second place...oh, I'm sorry," Adam said. "I mean, almost made first place," he said with a smile, which caused Samuel to blush with embarrassment.

"It's good to see someone who is persistent and will not quit when he wants something. The competition is going to be harder this time, though, with some new and old competitors like yourself trying for first place."

He continued talking as Samuel placed four coins in front of him.

"It starts in an hour," Adam said, "so listen for the bell." He pointed to two well-built and armed men to his right. "The entrance is over there. You know the routine; show them your ticket."

Once he verified the paid amount, he handed Samuel a ticket.

"See you in an hour," Samuel said just before turning to leave.

"Good luck," Samuel heard Adam say as he shifted his bow, which rested across his chest, to place the ticket inside his shirt pocket before heading back the way he came. Taking his first side street, he was surprised by a group of horsemen who almost ran him over. He barely made it out of their way as the boot of one of the riders brushed him at the shoulder as they rode by. The sounds of their horses' hooves had been muted by the noise of the crowd.

He was lucky they had been moving at a canter and not a gallop; even though with this crowd, it would have been impossible to ride at any other pace without running over people.

He was about to rebuke the riders when he noticed the black and green uniforms with the golden seal at the back; they were the king's guards, and he kept his peace. The riders did not notice him, either, as they seemed fixed on getting to their destination.

Samuel leaned over to nurse the pain in his right shoulder when a sudden sensation he could not explain overcame him. It was that warning feeling you get in an imminent danger just before it happens; he spun his head from right to left, but saw nothing.

The feeling did not go away as he tried to discern the cause of this sensation that was growing. That was when his eyes were drawn to four figures kicking something on the ground. It was in an alleyway some distance away that led to a dead end. Without thinking, Samuel started running toward the four men, pulled by some unknown force.

His heart began to race as he ran; suddenly, something inside him that he could not explain was ignited. The sensation grew until it completely consumed him with an unexplainable rush—not the kind that comes from facing an enemy in battle, but something more.

Afraid of what was happening, Samuel tried to stop himself, and like a dream, he could only watch as things unfold in front of him. The surge that ran through his body began to change him, and within a short span, he suddenly had clarity of mind. At the same time, the physical manifestation of the internal change left a silver hue around him.

His vision became sharper and he could see more than

what regular sight would permit. He could pick out little details around him as his consciousness was expanded. Taking off his bow and one of his wooden arrows, he pulled on the string.

"*A'shar-ta-nara*," he said in a voice and language alien to him and released the arrow. Once fired, the arrow changed midair into some form of silver, splitting into four straight pieces.

The arrows struck the four men at the same spot on their thighs, and one of them screamed with pain, followed by the others who grabbed their legs in like manner. One of them glanced at Samuel, who was now about thirty yards from them, and the other three looked in the same direction.

Struck with fear of the approaching bowman with silver eyes and hair, they hobbled as fast as they could away from the scene into the crowd, holding onto their legs.

Samuel stopped where the men once stood, looking like a cat ready to pounce on any prey that passed by. Just as it had started, the strange energy that coursed through him dissipated, leaving him weak. The essence of life he'd felt had slipped out of him like a leaky clay pot.

He stood stunned, trying to gather his thoughts together when he heard someone groaning. Looking in the direction of the sound, he saw a young man crouched down.

"They are gone," he said as the stranger took his hands from around his head that he had been protecting from being kicked.

"Are you okay?" Samuel asked.

"Yes," the young man replied in a raspy voice, trying to clear his throat.

Samuel reached out his hand, and the young man took it and he pulled him to his feet.

Once on his feet, the young man started brushing off the dirt on his worn-out trousers. With the care he took cleaning himself off, it was obvious he didn't have much, that being his first concern.

His head was level with Samuel's nose and he seemed surprised, looking into Samuel's eyes as if noticing them for the first time. He took a step back.

"I'm not going to hurt you," Samuel said, taking a step back too, to reassure the stranger he wasn't going to cause him any harm. "I'm Samuel Wyman, and you have no reason to be frightened of me," he said.

"What is your name?" he asked in as friendly a tone as he could make it.

"Jayden," the stranger replied in a steadier voice as he returned to brushing off the dust on his shirt.

Jayden was of medium height and build, and roughly the

same age as him, seventeen, Samuel thought.

He could not help noticing how guarded Jayden was of him, even though he had accepted his help. It was obvious from his appearance that the young man was destitute; his clothes were worn out and old. But what was odd about his appearance was what he was wearing, gloves. Leather gloves on a warm day like this.

Jayden had a black spot on the side of his cheek where he was kicked. The bruise was not pronounced on his light-brown skin. There was sand in his jet-black curls and blood on his lower lip that was cut.

Using his knuckles, Jayden pressed his gloved fingers against the swollen area of his lips and brushed his tongue over the cut to temper the swelling.

"I don't mean to pry, but what did those men want with you?" Samuel asked.

"Those thieves," Jayden said in a vile tone, "and they claim to be guards. One of them took an interest in me when I came through the inner gate at dawn. Scanning my cart, one of the guards looked at the other, giving him what I think was a signal that I was alone before telling me to go on. I could sense...I mean, I saw both of them a few hours later following me, hiding behind the crowd, hoping I wouldn't notice.

"I was cornered here by two strangers, and as I turned to

flee, the two I recognized were right in front of me. Too close for an escape, I stepped back. They must have reckoned that the noise from the crowds along the side street would mute my attempt to scream for help, and I knew it, too. My only option was to try to talk my way out of the situation.

"'Where did someone like you get the items you are selling?' one of the men asked, pushing me against the wall. 'I know you folks along the delta don't have things like this,' he said squeezing my shoulder against the wall. I was about to speak when another cut in.

"Does it matter? He obviously stole it from some high Lord, with all the thieves that swamp the city at the time. We'll seize the rest of your stolen goods and pardon you this time, since we are fair-minded people here in Bayshia, but you will have to leave the city.

"Even with the covetous look in their eyes, I had to see if I could talk my way out of the situation, but it fell on deaf ears," Jayden continued. "They wasted no time as one of them struck me hard on the back of my head. Flashes of color blurred my vision as I staggered forward, and another punched me in the stomach. I fell to the ground, trying to catch my breath as a succession of kicks fell on me, and I tried to protect myself. One of them must have taken off the tarp on my cart and discovered that it was empty. He kept asking, 'Where are the items?' But I said nothing, still on the ground trying to protect myself."

"It's all over now; they are gone, and you should be safe," Samuel said as Jayden walked over to his cart. "You know, you are welcome to join us—that is, my father and two brothers—if you'd like."

Jayden was silent as Samuel continued, "You know the roads can sometimes be just as dangerous out there as they are inside the city."

"I do," Jayden said regretfully. "I do." His voice was laden with the sad reality of that fact. "Thank you again for your help, but I must go," he said, excusing himself.

Samuel wanted him to come with them, but didn't know what else to say, so he said the only thing that came to his mind. "We are at the Stone Hog Inn, if you change your mind, and you can have anything you want to eat," he said aloud as Jayden made his way toward the crowded street.

As Samuel watched him leave, pushing his cart in front, he thought there was something peculiar about Jayden that he couldn't put his finger on. It wasn't that he'd never seen a youth from the delta before, even though mainly older men leave the island to trade for the most part.

It seemed like he'd known this stranger all his life, but that was impossible, since they had just met. So why did he feel they were connected somehow? This was the first thing he didn't understand. The second thing was how open he was with this stranger; Jayden had stirred something inside him that he couldn't explain. He had felt strong and more alive during that short time than he had ever felt in his life.

Even more than that, he thought almost in disbelief, the bruise on Jayden's face and the cut on his lip was fading away like they had never happened.

"No, people don't heal that fast," Samuel thought, trying to convince himself that it must have been his imagination.

While Jayden's attackers fled in fear, Jayden did not appear surprised or afraid—just shocked that someone had come to his aid, even though he didn't call out for help. As these thoughts ran through Samuel's mind, he started walking back in the direction he came. As he took his second step, his eyes fell on an object that reflected from the ground.

Samuel picked up the object; it was an emerald ring on a silver necklace. He brushed his finger over the ring's smooth surface. It was the spot Jayden had curled on the ground as he protected himself, Samuel thought. He must have dropped it.

He ran in the direction Jayden went, trying to find him, but he was gone, lost in the crowd. After several minutes of searching, Samuel gave up.

"What am I going to do with this?" he thought and slid the

ring into his pocket.

"I wonder when he'll discover his necklace is missing," he said to himself. "Maybe he'll stop by the inn." Hoping to meet this stranger again, he began making his way back to the magic show.

All that had happened as a result of his attempted aid left him bemused. The competition he had been looking forward to and had trained so hard for was now of no real interest.

He wasn't sure he could talk to anyone about it, not while he was still trying to figure it out himself. The unexplainable experience was hard to deny and he knew it. And if he was finding it hard to comprehend, then how could he expect anyone else to understand?

Unaware of the time, Samuel made his way over to Elye, consumed by his own thoughts.

Chapter 8

Ladies of the Deep

Iseac and the Ackalans rode through the night and continued the following day, heading southeast toward the town of Tru'tia. It was a clear night on the second day and the moon was at its highest point in the sky when they stopped for the night, about a quarter of a mile from the main road. Tru'tia was going to be another full day's ride.

They had navigated through the densely forested area to this open space. The area had a few fallen trees, and on one of the corners stood four boulders that rested against one another, forming a jagged tooth-like shape. Iseac set up his tent in front of it.

Clearing a small area, they built a campfire close to one of the fallen trees. Horses were unsaddled and they settled in for the night. Several of the men sat around the fire talking, as images of their shadows stretched across the ground. While most of the men stayed in the open field, a few of them kept watch around the site, hidden by their cloaks in the night sky, away from the main group. It was a quiet night, and only the normal sounds of nocturnal creatures could be heard around the camp.

Inside the tent, Iseac sat down, crossing his legs. He placed the tip of his right finger on the ground and began the process known as yosterio, or mirror boarding. As instructed, he did this every night before going to bed, remembering the words of Gabram:

"While people go to sleep assuming their night will be safe, you must go to sleep knowing yours is."

Concentrating, he touched at the core of his mind, causing the amulet on his chest to unlace itself. With the crystal unveiled, he placed the image of a human at the core, which set off a vibration from his fingertip to the ground. He saw nothing out of the ordinary outside of the people in his vicinity, and with this knowledge, he lay down, closed his eyes, and was soon overcome by sleep.

As the fire in the camp died down to an orange glow, one of the Ackalans rode out from within the trees, passing the horse stand, which was several feet from the main group. He stepped off his horse before it came to a complete stop and rushed straight to his commander.

A few minutes later, Tremay rushed out of his tent with the same Ackalan following behind. He knocked on Iseac's tent, but did not wait for an invitation before stepping inside.

"Sorry for the intrusion, but I just got report from one of my scouts; over five hundred Agoras are heading our way, south of our position, and they are about three leagues from here."

"What?" Iseac thought, his expression giving away what he was thinking. Agoras hadn't been seen for over seven generations. These soulless creatures were in the form of a man. They had white bloodless skin with thin flesh pressed to their skulls. Their eyes were dead blue and had teeth jagged like the Se'monia fish. Agoras were fast and ate anything with blood. They normally hunted at night.

"At the pace they are coming, we can't outrun them, and the Agoras' vision is better than humans at night," Tremay said.

"True," Iseac replied, "but your men are no ordinary men, either. Another one of your scouts, I believe, is here with more news." Someone tapped his tent.

"Come in," Tremay said, and the man saluted with a bow as he stepped in.

"I have news from the field, Ashra."

"Speak!" Tremay commanded.

Glancing at Iseac, the man turned to face his commander. He spoke with a sense of urgency, but without any sign of astonishment or fear. He explained seeing people come out of flames that dropped from the sky as if it were a common occurrence.

While the Ackalans were talking, Iseac was already spreading his mind again across the area. Images of people like smoke flowed through his mind's eye as he scanned around them. People came from all corners. Three figures in the group heading from the west seemed to be aware of his presence; one of them, with his face like dry clay, turned to look straight at him from within his hood.

The creature's awareness of his presence took him by surprise, causing him to retreat. He immediately spoke, cutting into their conversation as Tremay and Ackalans turned to look at him.

"They are not just in the south and west of us, but also in the east. The heavier force is coming from the west, and they are just as far away as those coming from the east."

No one had to say it, as it was clear that they were been ambushed; somehow, someone knew exactly where they were, and they were coming for them.

Dismissing his scouts, Tremay commanded one of them to have the men ready to leave and the others to get Hildra, his second in command. Hildra showed up a second later, and Tremay explained what was going on and how they had been cornered.

A plan was formulated before they made their way out of Iseac's tent, and it wasn't long before the men were all ready to go.

Iseac could not help noticing how efficient the Ackalans were in preparing to leave, as if it was always their plan. If it wasn't for the horses, no one would have known they were ever there. Since he had no time to pack properly, Iseac broke his tent and hurriedly hid it between one of the boulders. The anticipation of what was to come, even after all his years of training and practice, still made his heart race, even though outwardly, he was calm.

Getting on their horses, now saddled, they rode south in the night sky. Based on Iseac's calculations using yosterio, he immediately started counting down the distance between them and the group heading their way.

A few minutes into their ride, Iseac gave the signal, and they broke into different groups with Tremay and Hildra each leading a team of Ackalans as planned.

They broke to the right and left of Iseac, fading into the night, while Iseac led his group straight, riding to meet what awaited them.

It wasn't long before they heard the sound of stomping feet, and they rode closer to one another in a tighter formation. Swords and axes were drawn just before their assailants came into view.

Once the Agoras were in sight, Iseac saw they were spread

across the plain, creating a wall of people that, from a distance, were the size of an ear of corn. A small group of horsemen armed with bows and arrows rode behind the wall of Agoras.

They launched a volley of arrows at Iseac and the Ackalans while others rushed to meet them with their weapons drawn.

Stretching his hands in front of him, the thumb of his fingers almost touching, Iseac recited an incantation as he spread his hands out:

"The crystal within I call to seal,

Cast the path upon the wind,

Hold the air as firm as seal,

Follow the path my hand will lead."

The air above Iseac seemed to stir as he spread his arms apart. The arrows that rained from the sky were suddenly deflected by an invisible shield several feet above them, even as they rode with Iseac at their head.

The Agoras, too, had spotted them at a distance and charged like bees to a hive with their weapons raised. At the distance, one could see their beady eyes drawing close in what looked like a fog of black smoke. Iseac held his quarterstaff firmly in his hand while loosening the tension in his body, and for a brief minute, everything was quiet just before it exploded into chaos.

An Agora rushed up to Iseac on his right and was struck down by his quarterstaff. The metal ring at the end of his quarterstaff cracked the creature's skull on impact. As it dropped to the ground, another Agora was rushing in to take its place. Iseac's quarterstaff was still in motion when he struck another one to his left. It fell backward, causing the Agora behind it to stumble. It pushed its dying companion out of the way, snarling as it charged forward.

The Ackalans swung into action, moving with grace and speed as they came off their horses. They moved in and out through dozens of Agoras, sometimes working in pairs, and Agoras died all around them. These creatures, however, were determined to overwhelm the Ackalans with their sheer numbers. Their thirst for blood seemed to mute everything else; for them, the death of humans was worth the cost.

A few feet in, Iseac jumped off Durack for a better balance on the uneven field and to be less of an easy target. He struck another Agora that swung at him as others rushed forward to fill in its place. Iseac's quarterstaff was in constant motion, like a wagon wheel spinning from a horse in full motion. Its rotation slowed only when it came into contact with an intended target.

Now all they had to do was hold on while Tremay and Hildra attacked from their flanks, hopefully creating enough uproar and confusion to give them the room they needed. They had a short window to get this right, since the other groups were closing in from the east and west.

As another Agora dropped to the ground, Iseac glanced up. At the crest of one of the hills in the landscape, he caught sight of the silhouette of several horsemen watching.

They did not appear to be advancing, and two banner men stood on opposite sides of the figures.

Just then the sound of the first horns went off; some of the Agoras turned to face it, as they had hoped. A few minutes later, the second horn went off on the opposite side, giving the illusion that there were more Ackalans than their enemy had anticipated. It created a brief confusion, as some of the Agoras turned to face the second sound while others kept their attention on the fight in which they were already engaged.

At the crest of a hill, a man dressed in full battle gear sat on his black stallion, watching as the battle unfolded. He wore a finely crafted black and gold alloy helmet that was woven at the end into chain mail that extended to his shoulder. His chest was covered in a metal breastplate. The breastplate was crafted in brass, polished to a shine. The emblem of a two-headed serpent twisted around the sun was on his left breast. His feet were covered by metal shin guards.

**************.

"I see the council still uses those fools to run their errands," the man on the stallion said. "No matter. By the end of this night, we shall have one more piece to this puzzle." He could see the Ackalans appear from the right and left flank of his men.

"While their futile attempt to escape is entertaining, we have more important matters to deal with. Rohac and Abojan!"

"Yes, my lord."

"See to it that the those who survive tonight swear fealty to our lord and master, and take care of any that don't," the man on the stallion said. "Now release the ladies of deep."

"Yes, my lord," the soldier he was looking at said before hurrying off.

As instructed, the soldier made his way to a wagon covered in a black tarp.

He untied the tarp around the wagon and pulled it off to reveal a cage that held two dark masses. The figures rose from where they were lying, their scaled forms expanding like dough underneath the night sky. They stood over five feet tall and had to hunch forward for their heads not to hit the roof of the wagon. The two identically scaled creatures looked almost bat-like in their form. Even in the dark, you could not mistake their eyes–black lenses that were wider than those of an owl as they blinked, taking in their surroundings.

Both creatures looked alike in every way and the only distinguishing feature between them were the gemstones that rested on their foreheads. One was blood red, and the other bright yellow. The wagon swayed from right to left as they made their way to the closed wagon door.

The soldier unlocked the barred cage on their approach and took several measured steps away from the door.

Once outside, the creatures waddled over to the man in command while most of the horses twitched nervously as they approached.

"Bring me the amulet of the Anamerian, and then do with him as you will," said the man on the stallion. The creatures blinked once without saying a word, turned, and took to the air, blending into the night.

****

As steel rang and blood from the dead and severed limbs stained the field of battle, Tremay called out to those in his company, speaking out loud enough for them to hear, "We are running out of time and need to get the Messenger moving faster before they catch up."

The Ackalans knew exactly what he meant; time was running out and the other groups would be closing in on them soon.

So they picked up their pace, moving in a triangular formation.

Agoras fell around them.

A strange uneasiness began to build in Tremay. He was trying to shrug it off, even as they maintained their pace, when suddenly two things dropped from the sky, landing several feet from Iseac. The gleaming reflection from their black scales could only mean one thing: "Ladies of the deep," Tremay thought in disbelief. He cried out, "Star formation after me." The three Ackalans closest to him did as he commanded, with two of them moving to the right and left side of him while the third stood in front of him.

So when Tremay leaped over his companions' heads, it forced the Agoras to look up, giving the Ackalan in front a quick opening to strike. They did this, picking up their pace even faster as they made their way toward Iseac.

Tremay knew Iseac was as good as dead if they did not make it to him on time.

Chapter 9

The Rising Shadow

Iseac felt the same thing at that instant and glanced up to see two creatures wrapped in shadow drop from the sky, landing with a thud several feet from him. Their weight broke pieces of earth and one of them landed on an Agora, crushing it underfoot.

With their winged arms in front of them barely touching the ground, they rose from their crouched positions, fixing their eyes on their intended target.

They moved slowly toward Iseac. As they did, something began to happen to their form. Like bubbling lava, the black tar that was their skin shift in and out of itself till they took on the shape of women. Both creatures appeared dressed in silky black gowns with the same color band at the waist. Their faces were unnaturally smooth and pale, with eyes that were black, like their hair, which was loose and extended just below their shoulder. Their faces were haunting, like those from a nightmare, and the only distinguishing feature between the two creatures were the gems that rested on their foreheads.

As they walked toward Iseac, an Ackalan charged one of them with his sword, swinging and twisting his hands with amazing speed. The creature that was now in the form of a woman sinuously dodged his blows and then rushed into him, pinning both his hands.

At that minute, Iseac could almost hear the Ackalan's heart beating as the creature slid her hand to his head and twisted. It snapped the Ackalan's neck as Iseac watched the man's weapon slide from his hand. The creature released her grip on him, letting the lifeless body drop to the ground.

Iseac's heart started racing fast, not just from exhaustion, but from the uncertainty of what he needed to do next. He had just seen an Ackalan killed in front of him, treated like a mouse attacked by an eagle. He wasn't sure he could fight his way past the creatures in front of him.

In the corner of his eye, he saw Tremay approaching with three of his men. They were leaping over the heads of the Agoras, trying to cut them off in the air as they made their way toward him; but, he at that moment, felt alone. It was like being on a stage, and these creatures were the only two present, watching and waiting.

"You cannot escape," one of the women said in a voice he could barely make out.

The other continued, "We know who you are and we've come for it."

"Give us the amulet," the first one said

"And we shall consider letting you live," the other said.

They spoke as one as if reading the other's thoughts, which allowed them to finish each other's sentences, Iseac noticed.

Their tone was the same–unnaturally distant and empty of any feeling. It sent a cold chill along Iseac's spine.

"Your demands mean nothing to me, and what you seek I cannot give," Iseac replied. He was trying to hold the fear back at the edge of his words, but his eyes were fixed on both women.

Concentrating, Iseac set off the amulet on his chest; as it came to life, he chanted a few words in his mind as one of the creatures spoke.

"You humans waste your meaningless life, seeking a greater purpose, hoping to become something greater than the bugs you are that should be trampled underfoot," said the woman with the red gem. Both of them pulled out black spears that appeared as if drawn from within the darkness.

They both moved with unnatural speed, blotting the distance between them and Iseac, and the one with the red gem thrust her spear at Iseac. He leaned back almost in a bridge, using his quarterstaff for support. The spear missed its target by an inch.

As Iseac rose from the bridge, he shifted to his left, pushing the energy he had gathered along the weight of his quarterstaff. As he swung his right hand out, he sent a solid mass of air in their direction. The force from the impact pushed both ladies back, leaving skid marks along the ground to the point where they stopped, but they managed to maintain their balance. Agoras close to them were thrown backward.

They realized he wasn't going to be as easy a prey as they had thought, and they both grinned at the challenge as they came back charging, but this time they gave Iseac no room for a counterattack.

They tore through walls of air that Iseac threw up to deflect their blows as they swung at him again and again. The first blow that made it through to Iseac came with such force that it pushed him backward. The impact slid off the metal ring on his quarterstaff, coursing through every part of his being. The blows continued to come faster and harder as he deflected or dodged while looking for an opening.

His concentration was intense, but his muscles were beginning to tense up with each contact as he moved. He barely deflected one thrust to his chest that cut him on the shoulder. He was getting weaker from every hit. He knew they had noticed he was slowing down as they continued their relentless attack. Blood was running down Iseac's sleeves that he didn't notice. A few seconds later, he got a gash below the rib on his right side; it burnt like hot oil under his skin.

Iseac was beginning to see double as he tried to maintain his concentration. He caught the glimpse of a spear heading for his throat, and he shifted his body, leaning to his right with his head moving to the right side of his shoulder. Before he could straighten up, he was hit in the stomach, losing the air in his lungs. He fell flat on the ground, releasing his quarterstaff. Like a fish out of water, Iseac gasped for air as blood spotted his nose.

If this was the end, he thought, then he was going to take the first one that came close enough to him with his last breath.

One of the women walked over to him. Looking down at Iseac, she raised her spear to finish him, but a flash of silver blade shot up from the ground past her. She squealed and part of her body morphed, changing back and forth from its original form as it tried to grab its throat.

A silver blade suddenly protruded and retracted from the creature's stomach, leaving the area dripping with a dark liquid that was its blood. It dropped face down to the ground beside Iseac.

Still on the ground, Iseac turned his head to see where the creature's companion was, but it too had dropped to the ground.

They were linked...somehow, he thought, even in the fog

beginning to cloud his mind. He could see Tremay standing where the creature once was, with the same dark liquid sliding down his blade.

A voice that sounded distant, but yet familiar, called, as everything around him slowed down. He was tired and opened his eyes intermittently. He saw Tremay, tall and muscular with his dark face glowing, the silver lining around his pupil more pronounced. Both braids, which extended over his sideburns to his shoulder, waved in the air as he rushed over to him, with his horse, Durack, by his side. Tremay's facial expression was that of deep concern, and Iseac's mind wandered off again. He needed to rest...just for a minute, so he closed his eyes.

****

"Juab and Mosley!" Tremay called as he laid Iseac on Durack.

Around Iseac's mouth beginning to froth.

"See that he makes it to Tru'tia as fast as you can." Tremay said as he secured Iseac on the saddle. "The spear had something on it and it is killing him. Now go," he said once Iseac was secured. "We'll hold them off...now hurry!"

Sending their horses into a gallop, Juab and Mosley made their way toward a sparsely forested area for cover, but it was too late. A volley of arrows was launched toward them.

Tremay turned to face the direction from where the arrows

were launched. He could see Golans, with their faces painted for war, restringing their bows, led by a person he could not clearly see; the face was hidden by a hooded cloak.

"Kill them all," the man in the hooded cloak said to his men as they rushed toward the Ackalans. "Victory shall be ours this night," the man leading the Golans said.

****

The sound of the continuing fight could be heard at a distance as Mosley rode away. Durack was tied behind Mosley's horse, with Iseac's dangling body. Juab had fallen from the wound he took protecting Iseac from the volley of arrows that was aimed at them. He had taken one through his heart, while Mosley had an arrow sticking out from his shoulder close to his chest. Golans rarely miss their target.

****

When Iseac opened his eyes again, he rushed to his feet, ready to fend off any attacker, but none came. After a few minutes looking around, he relaxed a bit, still vigilant. His quarterstaff was gone and he did not recognize the place. It was not where he was a few minutes ago. He remembered being stabbed and should have felt pain from his wounds, but they were also gone. Silence was all around him like a still pond at the crack of dawn.

He stood alone in a forest he did not recognize, covered by

towering trees with their tops hidden by fog. The fog also prevented him from seeing far in front; from the way the air felt, Iseac knew it would be a few hours before sunrise.

"What is this place?" he wondered, "and what happened to everyone?" Was he dead, or did they abandon him in the chaos? He needed to find answers.

With little visibility, he tried to find his way, casting a spell that pushed the fog around him some distance. Each time, it slowly moved back, enveloping him again as he moved cautiously.

Iseac gave up on the idea of pushing the fog around him after a while, and with poor visibility, he tripped over the root of a fallen tree, but caught himself. He turned to see most of the roots sticking out from the ground. He decided to follow the tree to its head. He found a branch that was long and thin enough that he could break off, which he did.

"No more surprises," he said to himself.

The stick was long enough to use as a guide in the fog; however, what he really needed now was to find out where he was, and maybe a trail.

The place was still unusually quiet, missing the normal sounds of creatures roaming about. Placing the branch to the ground, Iseac sat down, crossing his legs. Concentrating, he spread his mind across the area and felt nothing. "Where I'm

I?" he said, becoming a little more anxious. Not wanting to think of how he got here in the first place, he tried again.

With an intense concentration, he reached out his mind as far as he could; like a sling pulled to its breaking point, he held it for as long as he could. And then he suddenly felt something; as he focused on it, the earth in the area rose, and a creature stuck its head out from the ground. When it was completely out of its hole, it spread its wings. A few seconds later, another popped its head out, and soon more started breaking out from the ground.

The area was covered with Rhanago, or winged serpents, as they were more commonly known, and Iseac panicked. These creatures were black as hatchlings, with coarse fur that changed to red and brown once they reached full maturity, growing up to four feet in length, with their tails extending about five feet. They had beady red eyes, with ears tucked above their head and six bird-like legs with sharp claws, three on each side of its upper body. A family of Rhanago was known to skin a deer to the bone in minutes, and they were always hunting if they weren't hibernating.

That was why there was nothing here, Iseac realized. Rushing to his feet, he cast another spell, swiping the ground behind him with a blast of air powerful enough to cut off any Rhanago that had its head out of the ground. Those that survived took to the air, following his scent.

****

Back in the woods, Mosley rode stooped on his horse. His vision was fading in and out from the loss of blood, but he hung on. Suddenly, a gust of air blew around Iseac's flopping body. This startled Durack, and the horse ran ahead of Mosley's mare, jerking him on his saddle. Mosley held on, but just long enough for Durack, whose rein was tied to his saddle, to calm down. Then he blacked out.

****

Lord Almaric, who had been watching the battle against the Ackalans, could see them tactfully retreating.

Not pleased with the failure of the ladies of the deep, he sent for one of his trackers. He wasn't going to remain on the sideline.

"I want half of the men to remain here in support of Ranulf and Asa," Almaric commanded. This was to support the men coming from the east and west. "And I'll need a full report when I return," he said to one of the high-ranking officers who was to remain with a portion of the army.

He, on the other hand, was going to take a smaller group of men to catch up with the Messenger and retrieve the amulet.

They took off on their horses in the same direction as Juab and Mosley, led by Lord Almaric, his tracker riding ahead of him with his men following behind in a single file down the slope.

Once they were at the location where Juab and Mosley were last seen, the tracker got off his horse and, while holding unto his horse's rein, walked over to a spot on the ground. He examined the area for a second and then turned to Almaric.

"One or two of the three have been injured badly, based on the blood in this spot and also on that branch," he said, pointing to a broken branch. "The rider will not make it very far if they don't stop to attend to his injury."

He walked over to another spot, following something on the ground and stopped, bending down to pick up a twig. He discarded it after a quick sniff and turned to face Lord Almaric for a decision.

"Knowing that one of the two people they were after was badly injured did not make any difference to him. An Ackalan was just as deadly in his dying bed as one badly injured; and seeing them with the Anamerian, he knew that only death would break them from their preposterous oath to protect him. What to do?" Almaric thought as he sat on his horse weighing his options. After a second, he looked straight at his men; he'd made his decision.

Chapter 10

A Messenger's Vision

Elena ran through the back gate, sending it swinging behind her as she made her way into the building. The rainy season seemed to have lasted longer than most years she could remember. Taking off her wet shoes and cloak, as was custom, she hurried up the stairs, lifting her dress over her ankles to give herself some room to run.

She ignored the turned heads and eyes that followed her briefly at her entry. People with family members under care gathered in the foyer talking as she made her way up several flights of stairs. Along the balcony, she walked past two closed doors to her right and stopped three feet from the open door in front of her. Taking a deep breath, she stepped forward, parting the curtain that draped the doorway.

The room was quiet, with Berta the earth healer sitting on the right side of the bed where Iseac lay while his parents, Rita and Lenard, sat on the opposite side; both parties looked up to see her walk in.

A sense of anguish suddenly overcame Elena, breaking her composure as she stared at Iseac, overcome with dread. So it was true that he was dying.

Rita walked over to Elena as she stood by the door, staring at Iseac. She placed her arm over Elena's shoulder and escorted her out of the room.

"Is he going to be all right?" Elena asked, finally finding her voice.

"Yes, child," Rita replied. "He's going to be fine now. All he needs is rest."

"I want to see him; I want to be with him when he awakens."

"You can," Rita, cutting in before Elena could say another word, "as long as you promise to make sure he doesn't move much when he awakes."

Lenard stepped out of the room and bowed his head slightly in greeting.

"*Kru haya no-nah*, Elena," Rita said in their native tongue, which means "peace and prosperity."

Elena's fear of the worst was still abating as she responded in like manner.

"We should leave now," Lenard said to his wife as she gave Elena a hug.

"I know he will be pleased to see you," Rita said, letting go.

Lenard was waiting as Rita came to join him, and they made their way downstairs. Elena, now feeling more reassured, made her way back into the room.

She sat by Iseac's bedside, whose arms, shoulders, and just above his chest was naked. The rest of his body was covered by a blanket.

There was a piece of cloth wrapped around his head, his eyes closed. His face was solemn and peaceful, and this was the man she was supposed to be betrothed to.

"He is a strong man." The familiar voice of Berta came from the opposite side of the bed, breaking Elena's chain of thoughts.

"I was able to set his broken bones and applied an ointment that will heal his wound. I also gave him something to help ease his pain and bring down his fever; the rest is up to him now."

"*Ma-u arura*," Elena said, which means "I'm grateful."

"How long have you had him in your care?"

"Since last night," Berta replied. "He was found by what used to be Ahyoo farm past Lake Manori."

The farmland was no longer well maintained by its new owner and was covered in weeds.

"He was lying on a black horse."

"Durack," Elena muttered as Berta continued to speak.

"He had cuts on both sides of his body by something that left a strange residue on his flesh that I had to clean out." She turned to look at Iseac and, as if talking to herself, said,

"Whatever Iseac has gotten himself into, let us hope he can get himself out, as it appears he did something worth taking his life." She did not mention the arrows she removed from him were Golans'.

A Golan's arrow was designed to break inside its target; it had four claws like tentacles behind the arrow head, which broke easily if one was not careful. It was tricky, but Berta had done it.

"The good news is he's gone through the worst part and will recover with time."

Though the words were comforting to hear, Elena could not help wondering how Iseac ended up in this state.

Berta continued to speak. "His horse was tied to an Ackalan named Mosley, who is next door. He too was lying on his horse with two arrows sticking out of him, one in his chest and the other in his leg. He was unconscious as well when he was found."

"An Ackalan," she said, somewhat surprised, but doubtful.

"Yes," Berta replied. "He sounds like one of the men from the east."

Berta was above her middle years based on the season's cycle, around fifty-six years. She had her hair tied in a knot and her sleeves rolled up just below her elbows.

"I will be back before midday to check on him," she said as

she rose from her chair. "The maids will bring some soup for him in the morning, if he has the strength to eat, and also something for you, my child, if you are staying through the night."

Something about Berta's tone was reassuring; Elena knew it was going to be all right because she said so. Berta placed one hand on the side of the bed, eyes staring at Iseac.

"I still remember him as a boy. Now he carries the weight only his kind can, which cannot be shared," Berta commented as if speaking about some stranger.

Her words made no sense to Elena, but she did not care; the only thing that mattered was that he was going to be okay.

She watched Berta walk out of the room, closing the curtain behind her.

It had been almost four years since she last saw him. Iseac never sent any message or tried to contact her. All of a sudden here he was, back from who knows where, half dead. She stared at his face; it was not the face of the young man she could remember from a few years ago. His face was harder and more intent.

"Where have you been, and why are men after you?" she wondered. As she took Iseac's hand and squeezed it gently, his eyes shifted then behind his closed eyelids.

****

Iseac was running as fast as his legs would take him, trying to put some distance between him and the squalling sound of the Rhanagos that drew closer and closer. While he was running, he spotted a speck of light through the trees, so he changed direction and started running toward the light, which slowly grew the closer he got. Rhanagos avoided the sun, so he knew that once in the light, he would be safe. As the relief of finding an exit was kindled, something snagged his feet, sending Iseac to the ground. He was able to cushion his fall by placing his hands in front of him, which saved him from more than the little cuts he received on his cheek and palm. Those didn't matter. He could see the sky and the field of grass between the trees a few feet away. He continued on all fours and was jerked back.

Iseac broke out in a cold sweat, realizing his leg was tangled by some vines. He focused on getting his foot free while trying to ignore the chirping sound that was getting close.

With shaking nerves, Iseac hurriedly untangled his leg, but the Rhanagos were already on him. They dove straight for him like bees to their hive as he waved his hand in the air, creating a shield of wind. Like drops of rain, they hit it, claws and teeth exposed as they tried to claw their way to him.

Iseac hurried out into the open field and, while still trying to catch his breath, looked back more than once to make sure none came through. He moved away from their eerie chirping as he could hear their beating wings around the edge of daylight.

A gentle breeze brushed over the open field of rich green grass higher than Iseac's knee, which was illuminated by the morning sun. He walked along the grassy plain with his path closing behind him until he got to a point where there was a steep drop. That was when he realized where he was–on a mountain overlooking the city of Bayshia, which he recognized immediately by the great wall.

Like an eagle, Iseac's vision became sharper, as if the city was drawn close to him. He could see faces clearly as one standing next to another. When he looked around, he found himself in the midst of the people. As he moved through the crowd, he caught a flicker of light at the corner of his eye. It was bright enough even in daytime to get his attention, and it didn't go away. No one else appeared to have noticed. The glow was like a candle in the middle of a dark room, and he was close to it. Curious, Iseac made his way to the general area as faces flowed past him like the wind. He stopped at the corner of one of the buildings and peeked.

Standing in the alleyway, covered by a silver aura, was a young man with a bow in one hand. The impression of the aura around the young man sent flashes of Iseac's dream to his mind. He pulled his head back and leaned against the wall in disbelief. After a second, he took another peek, but this time with a little more caution. Another person stood next to the one with the bow and arrow; this person seemed to illuminate the first. Iseac somehow knew that the second individual whose hands were glowing through his gloves was just as powerful. He couldn't see the face of the second person, as his back was toward him, nor could he hear their conversation, even though he could tell that they were talking.

He needed to get closer to hear what they were saying, but even more than that, he wanted to find out who the second person was. He looked around and spotted a building that was closer. "Perfect," he thought. It would provide the cover he needed. Iseac quietly withdrew from his hiding place. When he thought he was far away and would not be heard, he started running to the new location. Halfway to the next building, everything around him suddenly started pulling away. The harder he ran, the stronger the force became, until he was pulled into the air. Desperate, Iseac tried to grab unto anything he could find, but there was nothing. He turned midair, facing a ball of light as he was pulled higher and faster into the sky.

Everything became a blur, and he closed his eyes.

****

Squinting, Iseac opened his eyes as his bleary vision slowly came to focus. Looking down on him, shaded by the light behind her, was a woman he couldn't clearly see.

"How do you feel?" she asked in the gentle tone used by caregivers to a patient. She moved to his side and propped the pillow behind him.

"Fine," Iseac replied, his voice hoarse. His throat was dry and it tingled as he moistened it.

With his head propped up, Iseac turned to get a better look at the woman as she moved from the side of his bed to the corner of the room, but her back was turned away from him.

She began fixing something he could not see, but he could hear the clacking sound of spoon against metal with steam forming around whatever she was preparing.

Since he couldn't see her face, Iseac took the opportunity to look around his room. He thought the place looked familiar as he returned his gaze to the woman who was now making her way back to him. He recognized her even though she had changed from the young girl he once remembered.

'Gina?' he was about to say when someone else walked into the room, drawing his attention. The look on his face lit up in surprise.

"Elena," he said with a broad smile as she ran over and hugged him. It felt good holding her in his arms again. Her presence seemed to ease all his pain as he smiled back at her.

Iseac tried to sit up straight, not thinking of what he was doing. His body quickly reminded him that it was a bad idea as a jolt of pain ran through his side; he ignored it, clenching his teeth.

Gina, who was almost pushed out of the way, grunted under her breath twice to get their attention, and after another second of being ignored, she spoke up.

"Sorry to bother both of you, but I was told to ensure that he eat something as soon as he was up." Elena released her grip on Iseac and turned to look at Gina.

"I'll take that," she said as she reached out for the tray, which Gina gladly handed over.

"I'll make sure he eats everything and return it to you once he's done."

"Then I will leave you two alone," she said to Elena as she excused herself and left the room.

Iseac stared at her, amazed by how much she had changed. Her youthful mannerisms were still there, but inside was a now beautiful woman. Her hair was pulled back from her face, held in place by a yellow ribbon.

The last thing he remembered was fighting Agoras at the outskirts of Bremah and some creatures that took on human form. He was supposed to be dead, so how did he end up in his hometown of Tru'tia? As other thoughts ran through his head, he asked, "How long have I been here?"

"Five days," she replied in her so-familiar voice that felt melodious to him.

"For a while, Berta wasn't sure you would make it. Your fever took longer to break than Berta had thought." Elena didn't mention she had been coming every day to check on him since arriving at Berta's.

"You were found lying on Durack, with his reins tied to the horse of an Ackalan." There was a hint of another discussion to come.

"Mosley was badly injured, but he's well. The first thing he asked about when he gained consciousness was how you were doing. When he was told you were being taken care of next door, he got out of his bed and walked over to check on you, ignoring the protest of Berta and her maids, who were in the middle of removing the arrow in his shoulder. Your safety meant more to him than his own life, it appears.

"At your side, he asked several questions on your condition; when he was satisfied there was nothing else that could be done, he walked back to his room with blood dripping on the floor."

Iseac listened while sipping his soup. The first bite stung, as his mouth felt raw, and the sensation was no different as it slid down his throat. Like quicksand, it seeped into his bones, leaving him feeling warm inside. He continued eating, not saying a word, listening, until she mentioned a stranger who came looking for him the same night.

"I was told a group of armed men stopped at the Two Arrows Tavern, and another group came here. They were looking for two dangerous men who were badly injured and asked if they could look around. The one who led this group here spoke with the authority of a man who expected to be obeyed, even though he saluted Gina. This man she said had the accent of a northerner and the mannerism of a high Lord. Gina knew that regardless of what she said, they were going to look around. The only thing she could do was make them feel that while they were welcome to look around, it would a waste of their time.

'We've not had any new visitors as of late, but you are welcome to look around if you wish,' she told them.

"Even though the man she was talking to was civil, the one standing behind him had his eyes fixed on her. This man that stood behind his commander had no warmth in his expression as he stared fixedly at Gina with his deep green eyes while stroking the hilt of his sword, as if searching for a reason to use it. When their commander gave the signal to search the rooms, the men split into two groups. "The green-eyed man walked up the stairs, his hand firm on the hilt of his sword as he peered through the curtain on the first room, which was empty. The man cautiously walked toward the next room. He pulled the curtain open, and a young man, Dan, with his father, turned to see who it was that had entered their room. The man at the door stared at them for a minute and then turned around and left. As he withdrew from the room, a call came from downstairs. It must have been urgent, because he immediately ran back down to join the others and they left. What happened next was strange; Gina said the ground shook for a brief second after they left."

It was obvious they came for him and Mosley. "But not here," Iseac said to himself. This was not supposed to happen–people tracking him down to his family.

"So what would dangerous men like those want with you?"

Iseac looked at her for minute, gathering his thoughts. "I don't know, but I have a feeling they might be back," he said, not expanding further.

Not satisfied with his answer, Elena was about to press him for an explanation when Mosley walked into the room.

They both turned to face him. Elena's face was a mixture of concern and frustration, which she quickly changed, not wanting to appear impolite.

"I will leave you two alone," she said rising from her seat

and giving him a kiss on the cheek. Iseac knew it wasn't over; she would be returning with more questions, but at least this would give him some time to prepare.

Elena was sometimes headstrong, and this was going to be one of those occasions.

As she walked past Mosley, she bowed her head, greeting him in their native tongue, and he replied in the same manner. Iseac spoke up as soon as she left the room.

"We leave for Bayshia in two days; will you be ready?"

And while most people would have been taken aback by Iseac's words, Mosley appeared unperturbed. "You look like a beat-up rug; I'm not sure you are ready yet for the road," Mosley replied.

"I look worse than I feel. A good wash and some real food and I'll be good to go."

Iseac was loosening the band around his head as he was speaking. His body felt stiff and his side still hurt as he moved his hand around his head.

"What about your father and mother?" Mosley asked "They've been here, worried about you, since you arrived."

"I know," Iseac said solemnly. He knew how hard it must have been for them to see him this way. "I plan to let them know that it's all right."

He knew it was not safe for him to remain here for his

family's sake, but more importantly, he needed to get to Bayshia fast. He had seen the face of the first. While there were lots of inns and taverns in Bayshia, all he had to do was find the building where he took cover and start from there. Hopefully, he would be able to sense his presence when they got close enough.

Chapter 11

Why They Ponder

Elye was among the crowd exiting the show when he spotted Samuel sitting on the ground with his back toward him.

"What happened to you?" he asked, walking over to stand next to Samuel. "I told you I wasn't going to wait, but I waited. I was one of the last ones to go in."

"I was held up helping someone," Samuel said, turning to look up at Elye.

"For almost an hour?" Elye asked suspiciously, a smile creeping onto his face. "She must have been very pretty, then, for you to have lost track of time."

"No, it wasn't a girl," Samuel said, getting to his feet.

He reached out and grabbed Elye by the head, locking it under his left arm. With his right, he began ruffling Elye's hair as he tried to pull his head free. They both started laughing, with Elye tickling Samuel's side, and he let go.

After a few minutes of playing around, Elye reminded Samuel, "We better get going, then, before you miss your competition."

"Not this time," Samuel said with little interest in his voice.

"What?" Elye looked at him, perplexed. "You have been practicing for this competition for the last two years, and I know you are far better than you were before."

"Maybe..." Samuel replied. "But something more important came up."

"What do you mean?"

"It doesn't really matter now," Samuel said, not wanting to discuss it any further.

"Are you sure?" Elye asked again.

"Yes..." Samuel replied with no irritation in his voice. The competition no longer seemed so important.

"Well, if we aren't going to the Ramthon Flight, then let's explore the rest of the city before nightfall. We can start with the Homrie-Ale, the finest drinking house in the four Kingdoms. I heard someone inside during the show talking about three new flavors."

"That is fine," Samuel said, "after we visit the Porters Shack. It's on the way."

"Fine," Elye replied. "Let's go." They headed for the shack.

It was around dusk, with most of the shops closed or closing for the day, when Samuel and Elye arrived at the Stone Hog Inn. A wave of lively chatter filled the room with music, and laughter blazed through the door as they walked in.

The place was crowded, with visitors talking and drinking

as serving girls moved about with drinks. Quite a few people were standing because there were no vacant seats.

"Elye," a familiar voice called from within the crowd.

They both heard it and turned in the same direction, searching as people moved about.

Samuel spotted Faray standing and waving one hand over his head. He was at the corner of the room, trying to get their attention.

"Follow me," Samuel said, tapping Elye on the shoulder. They made their way to a corner of the room.

"I was wondering when both of you were going to show up," Faray said. "I was just going to give up fighting people off for these chairs. Sit!"

"Where is Father?" Elye asked.

"What?" Faray replied, the noise muting the question.

"Where is Father?" Elye asked again, raising his voice.

"Oh, Father, he's getting things ready for the ride home tomorrow. So, how did it go?" Faray asked Samuel.

"He did not compete," Elye answered before Samuel could respond. Samuel glared disapprovingly at him before turning to face his older brother. "Something more important came up."

"What? What could have been so important?" Faray asked, his expression almost mirroring Elye's when he heard the same thing, and just like Elye, he knew Samuel had been working hard in preparation for the competition.

"Nothing that I can explain right now, and besides, it doesn't really matter." It was obvious Samuel didn't want to talk about it.

"What about you?" he asked, trying to change the conversation. "How did things go in town?"

Faray spent several minutes talking about the mundane things he did throughout the day, but he had an edge of excitement in his voice. That was something Samuel had noticed since arriving. Faray was in an especially good mood, as if he were hiding or holding something back. It was good news, but what?

"Did he do it?" Samuel wondered as Faray told them of his day.

When he was done speaking, Faray said, wanting it to appear almost as an afterthought, "Oh, and I did it."

"Did what?" Samuel asked, even though he could only think of one thing that could make Faray so elated.

"What I said I was going to do when I saw Klair again," Faray replied.

"So, what happened?" Elye asked.

"She was at the side alleyway by the shop, restacking some crates when I saw her," Faray said as he explained what happened.

He had nodded as he said hello to Klair, drawing her attention.

"Oh hello, Faray," she had replied with a smile, turning to look at him briefly. "Father is inside."

"I know. I'm actually here to see you."

"Well, then, I could use some help moving the bottles in the three crates right here," she said, pointing to the crate she had stacked. Faray grabbed one of the crates and was glad for the distraction. It kept his heart from pounding while he gathered his thoughts, which seem to have evaded him after all the time he'd spent planning what to say.

"How is your family?" Klair asked.

"They are doing well," Faray replied, "and how is business?"

"Still busy, as usual; Father had to hire more hands in preparation for the crowds that were coming, so he had to cut down on his travel to oversee things here. But tonight we're getting things ready for Lord Alum's party," Klair said as they continued working.

"Come on. Think. Say something," Faray said to himself. "You can best most men your age in a duel, so why are you so worried and tongue-tied with her? You will not hear the end of this from Elye...now say something." He braced himself for whatever was to happen and opened his mouth.

"Klair," he said, placing one of his hands over hers to stop her for a minute. She looked up at him expectantly, and everything around him seemed to stop. "She is so beautiful," he thought as he spoke. "I want to be the person that makes you smile the way you did a minute ago," he said, looking into her eyes.

Those words made her smile again as she tried to stop herself, seeing that he was looking at her. She blushed and looked down, pushing a strand of hair back in place. She knew exactly what he meant.

"But Father, he–"

"I know I need to speak with him," Faray said, cutting in as someone else called.

"My Lady, your father needs you inside." They both turned to see one of Klair's family maidservants standing in front of the side door.

"I'll be there in a minute," she said, returning her attention to Faray.

"When do you leave?" Klair asked.

"Tomorrow morning...but meet me at the Stone Hog Inn. I have something for you."

"I can't promise that I'll be able to make it tonight. Father is expecting me to help, but I'll try." Klair kissed him on the cheek before rushing away.

Faray stood there, stunned with excitement after all this time worrying about being rejected. She had not drawn her hand away from his when he held it, and she had kissed him. He raised his hand to touch his face, grinning as he walked away.

Samuel and Elye listened, impressed with Faray; he finally did it.

"So what are you going to do now?" Elye asked.

Faray looked at him, his expression not slighting. He knew Elye's youthful exuberance sometimes got the best of his tongue.

"Well," Faray said, "I'll be speaking with Father to see if I can stay another day, and we'll see how things go."

They spent the rest of the night making small talk while enjoying the music performed by a man who played the flute, accompanied by a young female singer old enough to be his daughter.

They went to bed that night reflecting on the events that had transpired during their day. Faray had finally taken the next big step with the girl of his dreams, which, for him, was the beginning of what he hoped would be the start of his new life; he hoped her father would approve.

Elye went to sleep dreaming about the great magic show, while Samuel's thoughts were consumed by the stranger he had helped along the alleyway, a young man about his age named Jayden. He stuck his hand into his pocket and pulled out the necklace that held an emerald ring. It reaffirmed what had happened to him; it hadn't been a dream after all.

Chapter 12

The Prints of the Unknown

After two long days on the road, once setting camp overnight in the woods, Harold, Samuel, and Elye made it home to Chartum-Valley. Their father had agreed to Faray spending another night in Bayshia. He arrived the following day just past sunset, exhausted but bright-eyed.

It had been a week since their travel to Bayshia, and things at the Wyman were back to normal. For Elye, it was nice returning to his familiar surroundings and not worrying about traveling anytime soon. Faray, on the other hand, had been talking about a plan to go back to Bayshia. He wasn't going to wait for the next harvest festival now that he'd taken his first serious step with Klair. He finally spoke up about it during supper as the family sat around the table.

"I'm planning to take Klair as my wife," he announced.

Elye and Samuel eyed their father.

"Are you sure she is the one?" he asked.

"Yes, Father," Faray replied with an inflection of certainty in his voice.

No one said anything as their father stopped eating to look at Faray.

"She is a fine girl and will make a good wife," Harold said. Their mother reached out her hand, smiling with motherly pride, tears beginning to swell around her eyes. She squeezed Faray's hand, nodding her head in agreement with Harold.

Since then, things in the family in relation to Faray, though subtle, changed. Their father spent more time with him, as did their mother, as if preparing to send him off.

They were out in the field working when Faray told Samuel and Elye he had to leave.

"I have to take care of something with Father at Ruth's."

He was another farmer that lived several miles from their home. He was selling his old plow; Elye snorted under his breath, but Samuel heard it. He looked at Elye but didn't say anything until Faray was completely out of earshot.

"What was that for?" Samuel asked.

"You would think the wedding was tomorrow, with the way Father and Mother have been treating him lately. It's not like a gift of proposer has been given yet."

"True," Samuel said, understanding from Elye's tone that his concern had nothing to do with the wedding itself, just the change it was going to bring to their family's dynamic. "It's not like it's going to be happening anytime soon, you know. A lot of preparation still needs to happen."

"Well...I heard Father talking with Mother about going

back to Bayshia at the end of the season," Elye said

"You did?"

"Yes," Elye replied.

"I guess this means next year or so, you'll have two women fussing over you instead of just Mother," Samuel said teasingly. Elye face became flushed with embarrassment. He walked over to Samuel and pushed him by the shoulder. "No it doesn't," he tried to argue in his defense.

While there were the obvious changes going on in their family, there was another one that was more personal, brought on by their trip to Bayshia.

Even though Samuel had never mentioned it to anyone, his encounter with Jayden had aroused something in him that he could not explain, like the spark of a kindling stick. Since returning, he had tried to rationalize what happened to him as just a figment of his imagination, but he could not dispute the reality of the emerald necklace. Something did happen. He had held a power that was infinite and uncomprehending that made everything else insignificant. The feeling was still fresh in his mind after all this time, which was over two months ago.

His challenge, now that he'd agreed not to pretend it never happened, was determining where to begin. "How do you find answers to something you don't understand yourself?" This was the thing that was running through his mind.

It had been a long day and his family had just finished supper. Elye was helping his mother clear the table when Samuel announced, "I'm going to the lake and will be back by sunset." He waited to see if anyone else would be interested in joining him, but no one responded.

When Celina, their mother, saw that the others weren't interested in joining Samuel, she spoke up in that tone mothers use on their children, regardless of age, even after they leave home.

"You know, son, that I don't like you boys going to the lake on your own and–"

"Let him go, Mama," Harold cut in, not worried about Samuel. He was old enough and able to take care of himself. "And besides, the lake is lower during this time of the season anyway."

Before Celina could come up with another reason why Samuel shouldn't go on his own, Samuel hurried to his room to get his bow and arrows. The conversation had changed to something else as he made his way out of the house. He headed for the woods, cutting through their farm to save time instead of using the normal trail that led to the lake.

The clouds had been gathering through most of the day. As Samuel made his way, he looked up at the sky; from what he saw, he was confident that the clouds weren't substantial enough to cause rain.

At the lake, Samuel placed his bow and arrows by a tree. He took off his boots and tucked his stockings inside them. He then proceeded to roll up his trousers to his knees and did the same thing to his sleeves, which he rolled above his elbows.

He walked over to the periphery of the lake, carrying his boots with him and placing them by the edge of the water before dipping both his hands in. He washed the exposed parts of his arms, face, and feet, which helped cool and refresh him. Once clean, Samuel slid his socks and boots on and returned to the tree where his bow and arrows lay.

This corner of the lake was relatively quiet besides the sound of chirping birds, nestled or fluttering about between the trees. This place always provided the type of solitude he needed when he had to think.

Samuel stared at his bow, really studying it for the first time. He remembered his bow, like him, had changed as he ran to aid the young man called Jayden. The bow was old and had scratches all over it. A word was inscribed on it that he hadn't noticed before. Written in silver, it read, 'Lights Arrow.'

He took an arrow from its quiver, stood up, and aimed for a wild fruit high on top of one of the taller trees. As he closed his left eye to focus, he felt a slight vibration underfoot. He stopped and looked around. The trees gave no indication that anything had just happened.

"Hmm...must have been my imagination," he thought, so he returned his focus back to the tree with the wild fruit, but the fruit was no longer there.

Perplexed by the fruit's disappearance, Samuel decided to do some exploring. He had at least another hour of light, so he made his way into the woods away from the lake.

Falling leaves of golden brown and yellow covered the ground, making a crushing sound underneath Samuel's feet as he walked deep into the woods. He did not notice a pothole and stumbled over it, almost falling over. Irritated by what almost happened, he looked at the hole. "What sort of animal could have made such a strange hole," he wondered as he looked at it more closely, brushing away the leaves around it. The hole, he realized, looked more like a footprint. But what kind of animal was it?

Bending down to investigate, Samuel brushed his finger at the base of the hole. He looked at his finger; it was black. He smelled it–ash.

Now curious, he walked a pace from the spot, facing the direction he thought the creature or thing would have headed. He found another print, but it wasn't as deep. Whatever made this was big.

Other prints could be seen around the next one he

discovered, but they were too numerous to count. These newer prints were smaller and about the same size as a regular person, even though they were dwarfed next to the last print he found earlier.

Samuel noticed that the air around the spot he was now standing had a hint of smoke and the prints were still fresh, probably made less than three hours ago, from his estimation. He realized then that whatever made the prints could still be around and maybe even watching him. He casually crouched down so if he was being watched, they wouldn't notice any difference in his behavior.

Samuel listened for anything strange or out of the ordinary as he looked around. He quickly moved behind a tree, still crouched down, and then slowly retreated. Once he felt he had gone a comfortable distance, he turned and started running home as fast as he could. He did not see any prints on his way home.

The sun was setting when Samuel arrived at the farm. He felt something wasn't completely right, so he moved out of the open field. The crops on their farm were knee high, which made it easy for him or anyone to be spotted from afar. So he stayed next to the boundary of the farm where there were still trees.

Relieved that things looked normal from his distance,

Samuel stopped to catch his breath before proceeding, meandering through the trees. A soft breeze in the open field carried a charred smell that was distinctively different from the one rising above their chimney.

They lived outside the main town and had no neighbors for miles, so it was strange to smell something burning that wasn't around the farm. Besides, there had been no lightning that could have caused a wildfire.

Wherever this smell was coming from, it had to have traveled a long way, Samuel thought. While things had looked normal far afield, Samuel could see, now that he was closer to the house, that the horses and carriage were gone. That was not the only thing he noticed as he spotted the shadow of a creature too big to be a bird zipping overhead. He looked up to see what flew by but it was gone, the shadow disappearing into the trees.

As he was wondering what was going on, something tapped him on the shoulder. Samuel leaped backward, turning midflight to face whatever it was, in between his wordless shrill.

"Shush..." his father said in a whisper with a finger across his lips. "They can hear just as far as they can see."

"Who? What?" Samuel asked, trying to compose himself after almost being frightened to death.

"Come," Harold said, leading him away from the house.

Samuel followed as his father made sure they stayed out of sight, using the trees for cover.

Still not sure what was going on, Samuel stayed close to his father, who had a sheathed sword hanging on the left side of his waist. This was a surprise to him, as he'd never seen his father with a sword.

"There are two of them," Harold said softly when he thought it was safe enough to speak again. He returned his focus overhead, eyes fixed on their destination, as he continued to speak in a soft whisper. "They move in opposite directions, going back and forth, scanning for people who are alive."

What kind of flying creatures prey on people, " Samuel wondered as he listened.

"They came from around the lake and stormed the town, destroying everything along their way," he said, pausing for a minute, emotion weighing in his words. "My first thought was you." He didn't have to say anything else; Samuel understood then more than ever before that his father's love and desire for his safety was more important to him than even his own life.

"The homes and shops in town have been destroyed," Harold said sadly. "Since most of the people could not defend themselves against the strange army that came out of nowhere, they took for the hills, and the bat-like creatures that passed overhead have been picking people off."

"An army," Samuel said to himself, stupefied. "Where is everyone?" he asked, referring to the family.

"They are safe for now, and your older brother is keeping watch," Harold replied.

Harold looked up again to make sure it was safe for them to move.

"Now!" he said, running over an open field with wild vegetation. The grass brushed against their legs below the knees as they ran and stopped under another tree closer to the base of a hill.

Harold led the way as they climbed up the hillside, using the trees along the way for cover. The higher they went, the more sparsely forested and open it became. The ground was rugged with an incline that required them to climb on all fours.

There were boulders of every size weathered from their long standing. Some of the smaller gravel pricked Samuel's once-clean hands as they moved.

They stopped several times along the way, making sure they weren't spotted by the bat-like creature that scanned the hillside. "There!" Harold said, pointing, but Samuel saw nothing.

The rays from the sun still provided some light below the horizon when Samuel saw a narrow slit on a slightly bulging hillside that most people would miss from any other angle. It was a single boulder that hid the narrow entrance, and they were standing at the edge of it.

Harold jumped down, raising his hands over his head, his face inches from the wall as he landed on a ledge. Samuel did the same, taking off his bow and quiver, and not thinking about the drop at the edge of the ledge, which was a rolling hill covered with jagged rocks that rose from the ground like spikes.

They moved along a narrow gap in the mountainside. For several minutes, they had to walk sideways because it was so narrow. The air was heavy.

Samuel took deep breaths, trying to calm his nerves while moving between two solid walls that were a few inches apart from him. Their path was straight, even though Samuel couldn't see where they were heading in pitch blackness.

A flicker of light appeared overhead after a few minutes, to Samuel's relief, and the wall also opened up a bit.

Faray had his weapon drawn and was relieved to see that it was Harold as he emerged inside the cavern. He was followed a second later by Samuel, and Faray's expression changed into a big smile.

"Samuel!" he exclaimed excitedly, his voice audible enough for the rest of his family to hear, and they all ran up to meet him.

Elye was the first to run into Samuel's arms. "We were worried something horrible may have happened to you," he said, hugging Samuel even tighter with his head resting on his chest.

Tears were running down Celina cheek as she ran to embraced and kissed Samuel. Her son and the family were finally safe.

Chapter 13

A Town in Chaos

Samuel sat on the ground in the dark cave that was lit by the fire burning in front of him. The fire was little, almost a tease–a reminder that he would have been enjoying more of this at home. He ignored that thought, focusing on their present circumstance as he continued to look around. Samuel wasn't sure if it was poor lighting that gave the cave an odd shape in some areas, making it appear almost flat, like a wall. It reminded him more of a tomb.

He could make out old fire posts that were barely visible sticking out of the wall as they appeared and disappeared with the wavering firelight.

"What was this place used for before?" he wondered as he began to notice other oddities. His father had never mentioned anything about this place. First the sword, and now this cave. There was more to his father than the mere farmer he'd always thought him to be.

"How did I miss this place after all my years of exploring around it?" Samuel wondered. This thought was cast away by a more pressing question that loomed at the back of his mind.

He needed to know what happened to their townspeople

and to fill in gaps on the information he'd gathered so far. He knew the town was attacked, from what his father told him, and also about the mysterious creatures that flew overhead, preying on the people.

He stood up and walked around the fire over to Faray, who was leaning against the cave wall. Faray was deep in his own thoughts, like everyone else, as the firelight shifted in and out, revealing and hiding parts of Faray's features in the shadow.

He did not notice Samuel approaching until he said, "Has Father said anything about what we are going to do next?"

"Hmm...what?" Faray responded as he became aware of Samuel's presence.

"Has Father said anything about what we are going to do next?" Samuel asked again.

"No," Faray replied.

Faray had being thinking about it, too- a plan.

"I know we can't stay here too long, since we don't have any real supplies, but hopefully it should be safe by morning." Faray's last words were more of a wish than anything else; like the rest of the family, he hoped it would all be over by morning.

"So what happened?" Samuel asked in a rushed whisper, the eagerness in his tone obvious. "I mean, in town."

Faray was at first perplexed by the question, but it dawned

on him that Samuel had no idea what had happened; he had been absent. So he didn't know what sort of danger they were in.

"Father had gone to the smithy, and about an hour later dashed in through the door, startling everyone. He was breathing hard as he spoke, his face panic-stricken. 'The town is under attack and we have to leave. Get some food and water now...hurry!' For a second, we all stood there trying to process what Father said and when Mother moved, we all rushed into action, gathering basic supplies.

"Father rushed into his room and came out with a sword. 'Where is Samuel?' he asked, hoping you were back from the lake. It hit everyone then that you were still out in the woods, but before we could dwell on it, Father continued, 'I'll get him, but we need to leave now.'

"We gathered the basic necessities that we could carry before Father rushed us out the door. We were gone less than five minutes when we saw a bat-like creature heading toward the house. It made a high-pitched shrieking sound as it circled the house and then flew ahead. 'Everyone take cover under a tree,' Father said, 'and don't move until I tell you.' Once we made it here safely, he went searching for you."

"I need to speak with Father," Samuel said just before leaving. Faray remained in the same spot, watching Samuel as made his way to their father, who was carving a tree branch. He could see Samuel sit next to him and was in the process of having a conversation as their father picked up another stick and started carving.

"So what happened in town?" Samuel asked once he had his father's attention, and he told him everything, recounting the events that led to their current circumstance.

"A few minutes after you left, I took the wagon to the smithy to have the right wheel checked and maybe replaced. You remember the one that gave us problems on our way home?" Samuel nodded, humming a yes as he folded his arms to listen.

"The smithy was in the middle of his work when I knocked on the board to his shop."

"'I'll be with you in a minute,' the man inside said absentmindedly. 'Owen!' the smithy called to his son, a young man who was older than Samuel by a year or two.

"'Yes, Pa...' Owen replied as he stopped what he was doing with the grinder and walked over to Stan, his worn-out apron covered in soot.

"'I need this going for a few more minutes,' Stan said as he handed Owen the tong, which he held in place. Owen was a tall and muscular young man with long black hair that extended over his ears. He started working with his father at the shop as a young boy, and his knowledge of the craft was comparable to his father. When his father wasn't around, he ran the shop on his own.

"'If I'm not back in five minutes, it should be tempered enough,' Stan said as he stepped away. 'What can I do for you, Harold?' Stan asked as he walked out of his shop while taking off his gloves.

"'There is a problem with the right wheel on the wagon, if you could take a look.' I pointed to the area on the wheel. 'I'm planning to move some heavy equipment tomorrow. I need to make sure this won't be a problem.'

"'Of course,' Stan said as he crouched down with his hand on a spoke to look at the wheel more closely. Stan was a stocky man with dark eyes and thick brown hair with streaks of gray in his bushy mustache and beard. His arms were muscular and well defined behind the rolled sleeves that came up to his elbow.

"As he examined the wheel, Big Bart started fidgeting.

"Bento soon joined, and they moved their heads and feet with unease. They seemed troubled, which was strange for Big Bart and Bento. They are the mildest farm horses we have ever owned. I walked over to try to ease their tension, stroking and talking to each one.

"'Something is happening over there,' Stan said, pointing

to the plume of smoke rising in the distance. 'I wonder if that is why they are acting agitated.'

"'It looks like there might be more than one building burning, with that much smoke,' I said, once I saw what the smithy was pointing to. 'With that much smoke, I think they might need help keeping that fire under control.' Stan nodded his head in agreement. We decided to go and see what we could do to help.

"As we hurried toward the general area, which, from what we could tell, was around the town square, we heard the faint noise of a mounting crowd that was rising as we drew closer to the square. What was once the jumbled sound of an approaching mob soon resolved itself into a loud chaotic noise, as people ran past us, frantic and horrified. Most of the people were families with young children.

"'We are under attack! We are under attack,' some cried, but the town bells never went off.

"Stan and I looked at each other briefly, deciding what to do next as we were jostled back. We realized we didn't have anything to protect ourselves, so I started looking for anything I could use as a weapon. I found a piece of wood by the corner of the street that was about four feet long. I tapped it on the ground to make sure it was hard enough. Stan, too, was looking for something he could use to defend himself, and he found a rusting rod.

"'Well, this isn't much, but it beats having nothing,' Stan said under his breath as we turned the corner to the main street, the path that led straight into the square. What we saw next stopped us in our tracks, and for a brief second we stood in shock and disbelief.

"If this was a nightmare, it had come to life, and in the flesh was destroying the town. What we saw were creatures that looked like corpses with bloodless skin and cold blue eyes like frost. They had human forms, but willowy, dressed in ash gray and black. Hundreds of them, like bees in a hive, destroyed everything in their path as they made their way toward Stan and me. To make sure nothing survived, they split into two groups, with the second group coming behind the first to make sure nothing was left alive. Their monstrous facial features didn't hide their thirst for blood.

"The town could not be saved. We could only watch in horror as the invaders ran in and out of shops, destroying everything inside before setting them ablaze. Along the street were mutilated bodies covered in puddles of blood–people who were trying to flee or protect their loved ones just before they were struck down."

Those words sent flashes in Harold's mind as images of the man pinned to the ground with his son while trying to protect him flooded his memory. Their still bodies had been held in place by the rod that was driven through his back.

"Steven's butcher shop, the mill, and everything on that side of the town's square was set ablaze. They must have come from the southwest side of the town where no one would have been expecting anyone, much less an army."

"That is not possible," Samuel said to himself, as if trying to deny the fact. Everyone knew that side of the pass was dangerous because of sinkholes that lay everywhere. It was literally unusable. If they had used the main pass, with how numerous they were, they would have been spotted a mile off, and it would have given the town enough time to evacuate.

"They charged with a lust for blood, growling like wild animals, and in the chaos at the heart of the square, a creature stood watching," Harold continued. "It was large in size and tall, with broad shoulders. It moved slowly, taking everything in around him, shrouded in his black cloak. A little breeze parted its cloak, revealing a red lining inside, before it pulled the cloak back in place. The hood on his robe was over his head, hiding his face, but not its catlike eyes or gray skin with claws for fingers.

"Allan, who owned the shoe shop, did not make it. He was captured and brought to the man in the middle of the square, dropped off by the bat-like creature you saw fly overhead. The creature was black as tar and almost as tall as the hooded man in the middle of the square. Once Allan was on the ground, it took flight. The hooded man did not move, but pulled out a scroll from his robe, opened it, and showed it to Allan. I could not see from our distance what was on the paper.

"Realizing we too were in danger, I tapped Stan on the shoulder. 'We'd better leave,' I said, pulling Stan.

"'Yeah, yeah!' Stan replied, shaking his head out of his stupor. We heard a scream behind us as we turned and began to run away. As we ran back, we saw Owen heading our way with a half-moon ax in his right hand.

"'We have to leave,' Stan said, and Owen gave him a questioning look. 'I will explain later, but right now we have to be as far away from here as we can.' We started running again, with Owen joining us.

"'Be safe,' I said to Stan before rushing over to my wagon. I unbuckled one of the horses quickly and galloped home as fast as I could."

Harold remembered thinking as he rode home that he only had a few minutes before the bat-like creatures would be upon him and his family–if it wasn't already too late.

Samuel turned to look at his family when Harold was done speaking. What was going to happen now? he wondered. Elye was sitting next to his mother, gazing into the fire, while Faray was still leaning against the cave wall. The place again fell into silence, broken only by the crackling sound of their little fire.

It wasn't too long after he went to sleep that Harold tapped Samuel on his shoulder. "People are heading this way," he said in a whisper as Samuel cleared his eyes.

Samuel could see his mother, Elye, and Faray were already up. As he listened, he heard it–the sound of footsteps drawing closer. It was clear that no search party would be about this late at night, which meant that the invaders were still searching for survivors.

"I need some light," Harold said in a whisper to Samuel. "Grab one of the sticks," he said, pointing to the fire, "and come with me."

Samuel did and followed his father to the left side of the cave.

Harold took with him the two sticks he'd been carving, from what Samuel could see. The sticks weren't completely pointed at the tip, even though his father could try to use them as a spear. The shape at the tip was too flat, and the stick wasn't long, either, so throwing it as a spear would do no real damage.

A slope went down five feet at the corner of the cave, hidden behind a rocky mound.

"Here! Bring it closer," Harold said. As Samuel brought the

light closer, he could see a circular-shaped wall just wide enough to admit one adult.

It became clear to Samuel why the sticks were shaped the way they were as Harold started scraping the edges of the circle while he held the burning branch.

Speaking softly to fill the silence, Samuel asked "What is this place?"

"Actually, it's not just this place. Chartum-Valley, a long time ago, used to be a mining town, and we are at one of the mining stations. It's been abandoned a long time. I discovered this place as a boy."

"Why was it abandoned?" Samuel asked, the look of the place now making more sense.

"Wives got tired of losing their husbands working in what was a very dangerous condition back then. Help me push," Harold said, ending the discussion. The corner around the circle was visibly clean of the muck that was once around it.

Samuel wedged the stick into the mound behind them, and they both leaned back and pushed with their feet against the circle. It took several attempts until it finally budged. Slowly they pushed it in until it fell, making a thudding sound.

Harold had sweat on his brow as he turned to Samuel. "Get everyone over here," he instructed in a low whisper.

Whatever was outside was now directly above them, and

they stopped moving.

Elye was standing next to Celina, and Faray was standing alone, looking up. They stood frozen in their spots, listening and hoping the intruders moved on.

And then they heard it. Footsteps. They were moving again. For whatever reason, they had stopped, but now they could hear them moving. The sounds started to fade, but before they were completely gone, the branch that was wedged into the mound came loose and fell to the ground, bouncing off the hard surface of the slope. It made a single clanking sound before Harold caught it.

In Samuel's mind, the single sound felt louder than their town bell. Everyone held their breath and Samuel could hear his heart pounding, hoping the sound wasn't heard.

Samuel beckoned his mother and brothers to come over, and, as they did, a single zipping sound zoomed in through the entrance. It grazed Celina's left arm. She raised her hand to look at it when Elye, who was by her side, dropped to the ground.

Celina turned to look at him and screamed, seeing the final resting place of the arrow that had grazed her. It had barely missed her, but struck Elye at the back, protruding from his chest. The jutting tip was glazed in blood. Elye began to spasm as Celina dropped to the ground to embrace him.

Another arrow followed almost immediately as Samuel and Faray rushed over to their mother, pulling her and Elye away from the entrance.

A thudding sound followed a second later, reverberating inside the mine. Something had jumped onto the ledge and was making its way toward them, then another, and another, and it kept going.

"Get everyone out of here. Now!" Harold said in a raised voice, not caring if he was heard. They had found them and were coming for them anyway; he pulled his sword and ran to the entrance.

Fear and anger competed for Samuel's emotion as he stood there in shock. Faray pulled out his sword and rushed over to the opposite side of the entrance, his rage burning away the fear that once held him.

"If you want to help," Harold said to Faray, "see that your mother and brother are safe. Get them as far away from here as you can and follow the dampest parts of the cave. I'll join you when it is time."

"Now go, and don't wait for me," Harold added more gently. Faray knew he was right. He had his younger brother and mother to protect. Disapprovingly, he returned to Samuel and Celina.

Samuel could do nothing but watch his mother try to

comfort his dying brother. She brushed her hand over his hair, trying to soothe him. Elye's breathing was now in spurts as blood slid down the corner of his mouth.

One of the bloodless figures jumped into the cave, but since the entrance was narrow, it had no time to defend itself against the quick motion of Harold's blade that fell on it. It dropped to the ground as another rushed inside, swinging.

Harold dashed forward, bending down enough to flip the attacker over his shoulder, and piercing the monster's throat as it landed on the ground; its monstrous cries faded while others continued to make their way inside.

Faray pulled his mother away from Elye's motionless body as she tried to hold on. Samuel watched Elye lie peacefully on the ground with his eyes closed, as if any minute now he would wake up; but he knew this would never be. Elye was gone, and that deep sense of realization rippled through every part of his being. It threatened to drive him insane, but somehow, Samuel held on to a piece of his sanity that drove him into action.

Samuel grabbed the burning stick even as the image of Elye taking his last breath spun in his mind. He rushed toward the hole, passing his brother and mother.

He threw the burning branch into the hole and hurried through.

Celina was held by Faray, who was unsure what his mother would do, knowing that at this moment she would rather stay and die with her youngest son.

"Come on," a voice said from inside the hole said as Faray backed in after their mother. He could hear monstrous screams and the sound of steel blades.

"He has to make it," Faray said to himself, fighting the urge to go and help his father as he dropped down deep inside the mine.

Chapter 14

Undelivered Message

Iseac walked down the stairs dressed for travel with two envelopes in his hand. He placed one of the letters at the front desk before stepping out of the healer's clinic. The air outside was nice and cool as he looked up at the sky.

"The sun is going to be rising in another hour," he thought as he looked out into his once-so-familiar surroundings. Iseac closed his eyes and took in a deep breath of the fresh morning air. This place—his home—held so many wonderful memories of his past. He let the thought linger for a minute before opening his eyes again. In his heart, Iseac knew there was a chance he would not see this place again, but before leaving, he needed to do one more thing.

Mosley, who was already mounted, watched as Iseac got on Durack.

"Follow me," he said to Mosley as he sent Durack into a trot.

A few people were already up preparing for the day, and those who were out took notice as they made their way through side streets, staying away from the major roads. Soon they were on the main road, surrounded by an open field. They veered right from this road into a narrow trail, and fifteen minutes later, the wooded trail opened up into a farm. At the edge of the farm was a single house.

The home was lit inside, which could be seen through the window as they brought their horses to a halt several yards from the house. Iseac got off Durack, pulled the other envelope from his saddlebag, and walked over to the house. Trying not to make any noise, he wedged his second envelope in the door.

Mosley was watching Iseac from his horse as he did this; while he did not exactly know what was in the envelope, he suspected this was probably where Iseac grew up, his home.

"We head for Bayshia," Iseac said as he got back on Durack and they rode off, the farmhouse slowly fading behind them.

That morning, when Elena arrived at the clinic, no one was on the main floor as she looked around. She had begun making her away upstairs when someone called her name. She turned her head to look over her shoulder and saw Gina standing at the foot of the stairs.

"I have something for you," Gina said, moving to the shelf by the stairs. She pulled out an envelope wedged beside a bottle of medicine.

Gina had walked out from the storage room at the corner of the main desk, drawn by the sound of footsteps.

"He is gone...but he left this for you," she said as she extended her hands out with a sealed envelope.

"Thank you," Elena said behind a stab of anger at Iseac for leaving without saying good-bye.

"Is his room occupied?" Elena asked.

"No, it's still vacant."

"Could I have a few minutes alone up there?" Elena asked.

"Of course you may," Gina replied.

"Thank you again," Elena said and she made her way upstairs, trying not to appear too eager.

Once alone, Elena broke the seal that had her name written in front and began to read.

****

My Dearest Elena,

Words cannot express how marvelous it was to see you again.

The desire to stay that I might see you once more shook me to the core and threatened to split my heart asunder, for it will not be consoled.

I leave with this void and hope soon my path will lead me back to where it might find rest in you.

The course I now have to take I must take alone, as fate has chosen a different path for me.

My hope is that my presence here has not endangered

these people. I do not know when I will again return, and do not expect you to wait.

You deserve better, someone that will be there and care for you, someone you can raise a family with and live a normal and happy life.

I'm sorry for the pain I've caused you.

Iseac

****

Elena sniffed as she wiped off the tears from her eyes. There was nothing else on the note. She knew that Iseac was being trained by a Patron in Bremah, which required him to travel, but this had been the longest he'd been away from home. His knowledge and understanding of the four Kingdoms seem to ground him even more, and this was one of the things she loved about him. She enjoyed listening to him bring history to life when he spoke of events centuries ago as if he had seen them in person.

And after all this time away, he still held her heart.

"Mother used to say that men are hard to understand. I now see what she means, and even though she might be right, he is the only one for me." She folded the note and tucked it into her bodice.

After taking a second to compose herself, Elena walked out of the room.

Iseac and Mosley, on the other hand, rode through most of the morning. By midday, the clouds had gathered into a grayish blue; it was about to rain.

"It looks like we are going to be riding in the rain for some time," Mosley commented as he pulled his hood over his head, the wind carrying his words.

"Stay by my side," Iseac said in reply, not wanting to talk too much; his side and head still throbbed with pain.

Concentrating, he cast a spell, and the air above them shifted in a twirling motion. A second later, it settled into a transparent shield just before the first raindrop hit the ground and it began to rain.

Iseac pulled the hood of his cloak over his head and they rode at a canter with the rain bouncing off the invisible shield. This, however, did not stop the draft from the wind.

The rain broke through several times as they rode due to Iseac's wavering concentration, caused by the mounting pains in his side. Durack's continued motion exacerbated his still-healing wounds.

Throughout the day, there were occasional breaks from the heavy downpour; by dusk it had diminished into a drizzle, but Iseac didn't feel like spending the night in the open.

He knew there was a cave about a mile from their location.

The question he was debating was whether it was still there. He sometimes second-guessed himself when it came to things like the landscape. His knowledge of this cave could have been from a more recent predecessor, or over a hundred years ago.

He could see why before and after his unlocking, Gabram was insistent that he study the more modern maps of the Kingdom, which helped to confirm his knowledge of the past.

They veered left off the main road as Iseac released his spell and they rode at a trot through the woods that became more sparsely separated the farther in they went. They stopped at the base of a hillside. Iseac stepped off Durack and started walking along the corner of the hill.

Mosley recognized the place, but he wasn't sure what Iseac was looking for.

"Can I be of any help?" he asked, stepping down from his horse.

After a long pause, Iseac spoke as he continued searching for something. "I'm not…" and that was when he saw it.

"There!" he said as he parted the shrub that was hiding what he was looking for, a board that was old and weathered. It was the entrance to a tunnel that was about five feet tall, with a thick wooden frame mostly covered in dust and cobwebs.

Gritting his teeth, he kicked the board in, splintering the

wood around the area were his feet landed. Iseac leaned forward and began pulling off the remaining planks with his hands.

"We should be dry in here tonight, but stand back. "He motioned for Mosley to move to his right. When he was satisfied that he and the horses were a safe distance from him, he raised both hands over his head and moved his arm around almost in a circular motion. Something above him began to stir; as he swung his hand forward, a gust of air swept in through the entrance, making a hollow swooshing sound as it brushed the fore-walls of the tunnel, fading into the distance.

"That is better," Iseac said, rubbing his wet hands together as if cleaning them. His wet hair that had been pushed forward by the wind fell back into place.

Iseac was glad to be on his feet again; the jarring motion from their ride had left him sore more than he'd thought. Looking around, they gathered as many dry twigs and wood they could find–which wasn't much–and they got a little fire started, which provided little warmth. As they sat inside the cave away from the wind, Iseac closed his eyes and placed his right hand on the ground, the palm raised so only his fingertips were touching the ground.

Concentrating, he touched at the core of his mind, causing the amulet on his chest to unlace itself, revealing the fuchsia crystal within. Now that the crystal was open, he placed the image of a human at the core of his mind, which sent a vibration from his fingertips to the ground. The images of a human-like shadow formed within a fog that appeared in his mind. It returned no human form a mile around them, outside of Mosley, which it picked up immediately. All of this took less than a minute. When Iseac opened his eyes again, he began to speak, explaining where they were going and what they needed to find.

All this time, Mosley had not once asked Iseac where they were going or what Iseac was trying to accomplish. His job was to protect him, and nothing else mattered.

"We need to find a young man with dark brown hair and silver eyes that would be gray to most people. He might have a bow with him." Iseac went on to describe the type of bow and the inscription on it, explaining that the young man they were looking for was most likely visiting the city for the harvest festival and not a local, which mean he would be known by an innkeeper.

Bayshia was a large city with hundreds of inns and tavern. It was going to be like trying to find a spotted grain in a sack of corn, but not just one bag, hundreds. "I don't know the name of the building where we will begin our search, but I will show you when we get there."

It had stopped raining the next morning as they prepared to leave. They had a quick meal, got back on their horses, and rode west away from the mountainside.

Mosley was the first one to notice the charred smell in the air; it was faint as a result of the rain from the night before, but he could still smell it, and so could Iseac.

"Do you smell that?"

"Yes, but I don't see any sign of fire," Mosley replied.

"Let's head back to the road," Iseac suggested.

The smell of smoke grew stronger as they rode along the main road till they got to a junction with fewer trees. That was when they saw the birds flying in a circular motion ahead of them. These birds were red around the head and the rest of their feathers blue. Only one thing attracted these birds, and that was the blood of something dead or dying. There were many of them, which meant something terrible had happened.

The road they were on split in two directions. One meandered down to the left, leading toward Orie, and the other curved slightly to the right into Chartum-Valley.

While Iseac knew that every day spent on the road and not in Bayshia was valuable time wasted, the birds flying overhead were a sign that some might need their help. Besides, he knew a fast way through Chartum-Valley without losing time.

"Let's find out what is going on," Iseac said as he sent his horse into motion. The horses seemed more spirited with the sun rising as they veered right. The mountain pass, which looked whole at a distance, opened up as they rode toward it. As Iseac and Mosley got closer to the crest of the hill, the first sign of their fears was confirmed.

The birds were picking on something that lay on the ground. As they got closer to it, they could tell that it was the disfigured remains of a man in the center of the road. The birds around them flew a safe distance from Iseac and Mosley, their beady eyes shifting between them and the food that lay on the ground.

"It looks like it's been here about a day," Mosley said, judging by the smell as they looked down on the discolored corpse with flies around it.

There were arrows sticking out of the chest that they both recognized as Golan. The now-tattered shirt on the corpse had a symbol on it that flapped about, held by a single thread.

It indicated that this man was a courier, the symbol partially covered in dried blood.

Most small towns had a courier and a hawk used for sending messages across town, one confirming the other if there was any question. It also guaranteed that the recipient received the message. If the courier was killed by Golans, Iseac could not help but wonder what they could have done to the people of the town.

He urged Durack on until they were past the crest of the chasm. At their distance, they could see smoke rising from within the town as they rode downhill. No one knew why Golans do what they do, which made them dangerous, so they had to be vigilant as they made their way toward Chartum-Valley.

Chapter 15

Gone in Flames

The place had an eerie silence, stilled by inactivity as Iseac and Mosley rode into the valley. The scene was even more gruesome than they had anticipated. The acrid smell of burnt flesh and bodies starting to decompose hung heavy in the air like smoke. The streets on different areas were covered in bloodstains that stretched along the road from the rain the night before. Most of the buildings, from what they could see, were destroyed by fire. Their charred foundations were the only identifying pieces of the structures that were once there.

The potent stench turned Iseac's stomach and he threw up, unable to hold his meal.

"Are you okay?" Mosley asked.

"Yes, I'm fine. My meal just isn't sitting well with me this morning." Iseac wiped his mouth.

"I haven't seen anything like this before," Mosley said with a sense of horror. "Whatever attacked this people seemed bent on destroying everything in its path. With this much carnage, I don't believe they had any intention of taking prisoners."

"So what would Golans be looking for this far south, and why Chartum-Valley, is the real question," Iseac said.

"What did these people have that was worth destroying their town?" he asked himself as they made their way toward the heart of the town.

The sound of their horses' hooves against the cobblestones seemed louder in the silence that encapsulated the place.

Mosley continued to scan their surroundings beside Iseac.

Iseac got off Durack at the town square, releasing the shield of air he had held when they rode into town. There was a quicker way to check for survivors. He got on one knee, placing his right hand on the ground, concentrating.

This was the fastest way to detect life and help anyone that might still be alive. As images of the dead swept past his consciousness, he felt a single pulse, and narrowed his focus on it. It was not far from their position, but before he could say anything, he heard a splintering sound. He released his concentration, opening his eyes to see Mosley standing in front of him with a piece of broken arrow on the ground.

"Someone is here," Mosley exclaimed, his voice raised.

"I know," Iseac replied as he ran for cover.

"Golan," Iseac thought as Mosley took cover on the opposite side. He only sensed one; unless something had changed, there should have been more arrows aimed at them.

Golans were known to go in a pack of four, and only if the others were killed would you find one alone.

He needed to know what had happened to these people, and whoever had just shot at them was their key to finding the answers.

Looking around, nothing provided any real cover. Iseac crouched down against a waist-high stone wall, the edges charred by the fire that had consumed it.

"I will attack him head on while you go around," Iseac said to Mosley, who acknowledged the plan with a nod.

"And we need this person alive," he said as the air around him pulled itself into a solid mass in front of him.

"Now," Iseac said as he ran out from cover, rushing forward to meet their assailant, his feet barely touching the ground with his cloak flapping behind him like a flag.

Mosley watched as Iseac sprinted in the direction the arrow was fired, and he darted to his left, his eyes focused on the general vicinity where the intruder was hiding. Iseac caught a slight rustling in the woods as he rushed in, just as his shield deflected another arrow. That one had been aimed for his head.

He could not get a clear view of the Golan between the rustling branches as the Golan was retreating. So he ran faster to close the distance, bursting into an open clearing inside the woods. The sun peered through gaps in the trees, its rays illuminating the rich green and brown leaves that covered the open area.

As Iseac looked for signs of the Golan, he heard the swooshing sound of something zip by. He turned to face it, ignoring the sound of something slumped to the ground.

Iseac could see Mosley putting his hand down. He had just killed their only witness, he thought, as he turned his attention to the Golan, which was the slumped sound he had ignored.

"He is not dead," Mosley said confidently as he walked over to the body, joining Iseac.

"His head will be throbbing when he gets up, that's all," Mosley said, picking up his knife. He had knocked him out with the head of his knife.

Iseac pulled the hood off the face of the Golan and was shocked at what he saw. It wasn't a Golan, as he had suspected, but one of the young men in his dream.

"It's him!" Iseac exclaimed in disbelief. "The one we needed to find in Bayshia."

Mosley looked at Iseac. He had no hint of surprise in his expression, but his eyes showed that he was perplexed.

The young man's face had patches of dirt over it; his cloak was damp and dirty. He was dirty all over, with dried blood on his arm and lower ribs. Mosley stooped down and picked up the limp body from the ground. Iseac picked up his bow, and they walked back toward the town square.

That night, there was a stir as the young man rose from his

makeshift bed on the ground.

"Ah...our mysterious archer, how do you feel?" Iseac asked as if talking to an old friend. "Sorry for the bump, but that was the only way we could stop you." He watched the young man blink while shaking his head to clear it.

The motion must have been painful, because he placed both his hands on his head, which was wrapped in a woolen cloth to cover the wound he received from Mosley's knife.

"You'll find meat and fruit on the plate next to you, if you are hungry," Iseac said as he bit into his own food.

The young man said nothing, but instead looked to the right and left of him, past his plate.

"Looking for this?" Iseac said, his voice drawing the young man's attention as he placed the bow in front of him. The young man stared at Iseac, wondering what was going to happen next.

"Are they going to kill me?" he wondered. "If they were, then why am I not in a restraint?" the rational part of him said. "And why would they bind my wound?"

"Okay," the young man thought to himself, unsure what to make of his current circumstance.

"You can have this back," Iseac said, pausing for a second, "after you tell us what happened here first." The young man stared at him, somewhat confused.

"Do you have a name?" Iseac asked.

"Yes," he muttered after a minute.

"I'm Iseac, and he is Mosley," he said, gesturing to the Ackalan, who nodded his head in salute before sitting down. "You now have our names, but I don't believe we got yours."

"Samuel," the young man replied with some reservation as he stared at Iseac, who appeared to be about the same age as Faray. This thought sparked feelings of anger and sadness as he remembered seeing Faray lying on a wagon, bloody. He needed to get out of here and find his family. Iseac's words cut in on his thoughts.

"Well, Samuel, why don't you get something to eat?"

Iseac needed to get Samuel to relax, so he began to speak.

"We were heading to Bayshia and decided to stop by the valley for some supplies. When we arrived, we were shocked to see the town destroyed and all the people killed. We were searching for survivors when you showed up."

Samuel listened as his head slowly shifted from a throb to a dull ache, with his eyes adjusting to the firelight that danced several feet from him.

As his senses returned, the aroma of what was cooking over the fire pricked his hunger. He remembered Iseac saying something about food being next to him.

He picked up the plate and placed it on his lap. "If they

were going to kill me," he thought, "they wouldn't have gone through this trouble." And there was a sense of honesty and openness about the man who called himself Iseac.

He took his first bite and waited. Nothing happened.

It tasted so good. Without knowing it, he began to eat with the ferocity of a hungry wolf, unaware of the silence in the camp.

"Would you like some more?" he heard Iseac ask as he looked to see them watching him.

"No, I'm fine," he said, slightly embarrassed as he tried to tame his protesting stomach.

"Here, have a drink," Iseac said as he tossed him the skin he was drinking from.

"I know this must be difficult, but what happened here?" Mosley asked as Samuel corked the lid back on the skin. "I have never seen this much carnage outside of a battlefield, and not with women and children, either. The people of the town seem to have been caught unaware. What I don't understand is how so many people could have appeared without anyone spotting them miles before they came upon the town."

"They came from the southwest side of the town," Samuel caught himself saying. "They somehow knew no one would be expecting an army from that direction.

"It is a treacherous area that has taken the lives of many;

few people use it because of its many pitfalls. How they managed to get so many through, I don't know."

"An army?" Mosley asked. "What did they look like? What were they wearing?"

"They weren't really humans; they had pale white skin like corpses, with deep blue bulging eyes, and their teeth were jagged. Another group with red paint over the right side of their faces carried bows. They were accompanied by two bat-like creatures, which is the only way I can describe them. The creatures were taller than an average man and black as tar. They searched the hillside, killing the people that survived the initial raid.

"Those who were not killed were taken captive," he said, pausing to hold back the tears that slid down his cheeks. "My brother and mother were taken, too."

"How did you escape?" Iseac asked, seeing the pain in Samuel's face.

"My father knew of an entrance into the mines," he said, sniffling, "and he took us there while the town was under attack, hoping that once it was safe, we would head to the nearest town. We hid there until they found us the same night. I lost my younger brother that day as my father defended the entrance, giving us a chance to run farther into the mine; he never joined us.

"They came after me, my brother, and mother as we ran deep into the mines, and it wasn't long before we could hear their growling sounds behind us as they drew closer and closer. We knew they were going to catch up before we made it out of the mines, so I had my older brother, who was very good with the sword, take my mother with him while I tried to slow them down long enough for them to escape."

Samuel remembered this caused some argument, most especially with his mother, who didn't want him to stay behind, but he and Faray knew it was their best chance of getting out alive. Samuel was good with the bow and arrow, more than an average archer, and they knew it.

"I hid behind one of the several mounds inside the cave overlooking the main pass and watched my brother and mother leave, with their light fading into the distance as I waited."

Samuel remembered the raw emotion he had felt at that moment, thinking of Elye, and the anger burned inside him as he waited patiently.

"It wasn't too long before the flickering lights of our assailants appeared, their growling sound echoing off the walls. I pulled on my bow, watching as one of them came into view, and let go. The creature dropped to the ground from the arrow that found its resting place in its forehead, but the others kept moving, undeterred by their dead comrade as they peered into the dark, keeping up their pace. Two more dropped down, squealing, and I moved to a different position, the darkness providing cover. They did not seem to care as the main body kept moving, while others searched around. With two more down, they slowed their pace slightly, but kept marching across the wide chasm. I decided to move to the back of the group to try and draw them toward me.

"As I moved in the dark, one of them spotted me and pointed in my direction. Someone in their group spoke up in a language I could not understand and several of them ran to meet me, their drawn blades catching the dim firelight as they blended into the dark. I had my arrow notched as I moved back, listening to their growling sounds as they drew closer with an increasing speed."

Samuel remembered his sweaty palms and his heart pounding against his chest as he tried to watch his blind spot. Death was coming for him, and there was nothing he could do except face it the way anyone would trying to protect his family.

"Just then, I caught a dark figure at the corner of my eyes leaping toward me; I released my last arrow as I stepped backward, but I wasn't fast enough. I felt a sharp pain in my left arm and lower rib as one of the creatures tried to end my life. I turned and began to run, unsure where I was heading. Then I heard a splintering sound under my feet and I fell into a black hole.

"I crashed in, leaning forward, letting go of my bow as I fell into this abyss. I stretched my hands in the darkness, hoping to find something, and did. It was damp and hard, and I quickly held on. I was jerked to a stop as sharp pains ran from my arms to the rest of my body. They threw in several spears just to make sure I didn't survive, but I hung on. After several minutes, satisfied that I was probably dead, they left.

"My left arm and side burned with pain, and I was sure I had broken a bone. But I gritted my teeth and slowly made my way back to the top. Covered in dirt and sweat, bruised and exhausted, I made my way in the dark. Every step sent jets of pain through by body, but I knew I needed to keep moving. My family was waiting for me. I stumbled upon my bow. Maybe it was hidden from view, or the creatures did not care.

"I also found my last arrow, plus another one covered in blood. Armed, I slowly made my way toward what I hoped was the exit and was relieved to find that I didn't get lost. I approached it cautiously and heard a wagon roll up. I peered through the exit and saw people cramped behind bars. At the base of the wagon was my mother crying as she cradled my older brother, Faray, her hands red with blood. She was surrounded by people I recognized from the town.

"A large creature with gray skin dressed in a deep blue robe with a gold lace around the waist stood next to the wagon. It's back was turned toward me, so I could not see his face, but I had a feeling that he would pinpoint my location if I had made any sudden move. So I stayed, silently watching, my body slowly becoming numb. This creature seemed to still the wagon horses before raising his hand over his head.

"I'm not sure how to describe what happened next," Samuel said, looking down at the ground. He wasn't sure if it was a hallucination brought on by his wound, but he said it, regardless of what they might think.

"The creature wearing the blue robe raised his hand, and a tiny spark formed at the tip of his finger. It slowly changed into a fireball that expanded till it consumed everyone close to him. As the intensity of the flame grew, the ground began to shake, and they were gone–disappeared; the only visible sign of their presence was a charred curved ring burnt into the ground.

"I stayed there marveling at what happened, confused, tired, and cold, until sleep came and took me that night. The next morning, I was wandering in the woods, unaware that I was making my way toward the town square. That was when I heard the faint clanking sound of horses' hooves. I ran toward a tree to get a better view of the strangers that stopped in the town square. As I stared, wondering who you were, I felt you looking at me within my mind's eyes. It was like seeing someone at the bottom of a stream, even though I could see you weren't facing me. I panicked and fired, thinking they had returned to finish any remaining survivors they may have missed."

Samuel stopped talking and looked at Iseac and Mosley for some reaction as silence again fell on the camp.

Iseac stood up, walked over to Samuel, and placed his bow in front of him. "We are trying to stop the creatures that have done this," he said, "and we will help you find your family."

Chapter 16

Beginnings to Discovery

Iseac was lying down, still awake, as the embers from their campfire went out. He had found the first of three, drawn to this place by a force he could not explain, to find the only survivor was the person he was going to search for in Bayshia.

What Samuel told them confirmed one thing: the information they had received from Ditra-Vashine about the fire that consumed its victims without leaving any trace of their presence was true. The burnt ring formation on the ground, with the earth shaking, was also consistent with the report.

He had also felt something extraordinary about Samuel; unlike anyone he'd ever known, Samuel had felt him when he was using yosterio.

Iseac was beginning to believe that what happened here was no random act; someone, he thought, was willing to destroy this town and its people to find the same person he was looking for. Why and for what reason was still a mystery.

Iseac knew there wasn't much he could do about Samuel's family, but he needed to get him somewhere safe before continuing his search for the other two. He also needed to get some answers from the Council about this new development.

****

Samuel could hear Elye screaming as he ran into their home. Half the house was gone, consumed by a fire that was still burning. He could see the lifeless bodies of his father and mother lying on the ground in pools of blood. When Elye again screamed for help, Samuel's eyes followed the sound ahead of him, through the field covered in smoke. He could see the creatures from the mine pulling Elye into the woods, and he ran after them with his bow drawn. They seemed to elude him every time he got close, and when he looked again, Elye was on the ground. He aimed at the one with the spear who is about to end Elye's life, when the ground opened underneath him. As he fell into a black hole, he opened his eyes.

****

Iseac had been watching Samuel tossing in his sleep just before he jerked himself up with his eyes wide open.

"Are you okay?" Iseac asked.

"Yes, I'm fine," Samuel replied, wiping his hand over his face.

"There is someone that can help us find your family, but we need to go to Kadan's claw," Iseac said once he was done packing.

Kadan's Claw was on the southern corner of the Kadan River, which ran through most of the four Kingdoms.

Samuel gave Iseac a quizzical look; he didn't want to leave his hometown even though, in his heart, he knew there was nothing he could do if he stayed. Irrationally, he clung to the idea that his family would come back and that all he needed to do was wait.

Iseac could see Samuel's reluctance to go and said with genuine sympathy in his voice, "A wise man once told me that 'knowing your enemy is the best upper hand you want to have.' I know this is hard, but if you are to have any chance of finding your family, you need to first find their captors."

Samuel remained in the same spot, looking down, as Iseac continued to speak. "The pale-skinned monsters that attacked your town are called Agoras." Iseac secured one of the loose items on his saddlebag. "We believe they serve Sullivan, whom we suspect is building an army and planning to take over the four Kingdoms. What happened here also happened in Utorm, a small village in the outskirts of Bremah. Most of the people vanished after a slight tremor. A burnt ring similar to your description was found on the ground; it was the only thing they found when they tracked the missing villagers into the woods where they were herded."

This information got Samuel's attention; it confirmed that what he saw was no hallucination.

Samuel had never heard of Agoras before, or this Sullivan

whom they serve, but what was more suspicious was how this stranger, who called himself Iseac, knew so much about them. Samuel knew for now he did not have a lot of options. He would take Iseac at his word that he was trying to stop the creatures that had done this.

If Iseac knew so much about them, Samuel thought, then maybe he could help him find his family after all. He brushed his side and picked up his bow.

"You can ride on Kenda," Mosley said.

"What about you?" Samuel asked.

"I think I can manage," Mosley said as he secured the saddle on his horse.

The bay raised his head briefly to look at Samuel as he approached; once he was mounted, they rode at a canter toward Lufgard.

Samuel periodically glanced behind him as they rode, each time even more amazed by Mosley, who kept up with them the entire time. At noon, they stopped by a small stream to allow their horses to drink while they ate some smoked meat Iseac had packed in his saddlebag with wild berries they picked on the way. That was the only time they stopped until they went to bed that night. The next day was about the same, except that by the end of the day, Samuel had a nagging question. That night as they sat around the fire picking off the remaining pieces from the rabbit they were having for dinner, Samuel decided to ask.

"You mentioned that knowing your enemy is the best upper hand you want to have. Who is Sullivan, and why Chartum-Valley?"

"Well, concerning your second question, we'll soon find out; but let me shed some light on your first. Very few people know this, but a long time ago, before the formation of the four Kingdoms as we know it today, a merchant named Ryham found what is known as the first key of creation.

"Ryham was a good man with a pure heart, it was said. He was fair in his dealings and so was respected by most of the townspeople he dealt with. One day on his way to the eastern land called Millgran, he saw something flicker at the corner of his eyes. Whatever it was had blazed like the star, and even though it was for a split second, it caught enough of his attention that he stopped. Curious, Ryham rode his wagon toward the area where he thought he saw the light, stopping by the side of the road. He walked a few feet into the patched field and was surprised to discover a crystal gem. Its luster was something he'd never seen before, and even with the sun behind the horizon, the object glittered with breathtaking brilliance.

"Ryham stretched his finger out to touch it with the same

caution one would take when touching something hot; nothing happened. So Ryham picked up the smooth gem with its unusual shape, staring at it in amazement. It was a crystal rod the length of a forefinger, with four claw-like shapes on one end. At the core of the crystal was a silver-like flame that pulsated.

"As the crystal held Ryham's gaze, something opened up within his mind's eye. A door intricately designed with patterns of the solar system appeared out of thin air and was drawn close to him. The sudden appearance of the celestial door frightened him so much, he dropped the gem.

"Everything around him returned to the way it was, with Ryham alone and the gem gleaming on the ground.

"How Ryham's true self was revealed, no one knows, but we know he was the first Patron, and he found the first Anamerian, who formed the group called Ackalans."

'What are Anamerians?' Samuel was about to ask, but decided not to; he would do that later, he thought, as Iseac continued to speak.

"The Ackalans, at the beginning, were only known by the rulers of the four Kingdoms, bound by their oath as protectors of the keys or scroll of creation and its keepers. Before the end of his life, Ryham discovered seven more keys and the Patrons in the lands that guard them. The male line of Ryham served as Patrons for four generations until Graham, who had no son. His wife, Lenia, had Graham form a society called the Ryham Council, now known as just the Council. Graham's daughter, Rose, had a son. He took the oath and office as Patron.

"Rose's great-great-grandson, five generations later, had a son who was named after Rose's father, called Graham, and he had a son named Sullivan. Sullivan, as a young boy, was very curious, and one day decided to follow his father and sneak along. Graham back then was the Patron of the Mevi-tra temple in Bremah.

"It was a bright winter's day when Graham left for the temple, unaware of his son following him. It had snowed the day before, so even though it was bright, it was still chilly. Staying out of sight, Sullivan followed his father. While keeping up with him, he occasionally stared into the trees, distracted by birds that flew from different branches and little animals that roamed about looking for food; it was a beautiful day.

"However, by midday, Sullivan realized he wasn't in his familiar surroundings anymore; he was committed. He had to make sure he didn't lose his father, which he didn't, until they arrived at the temple entrance.

"Sullivan watched his father go in as he hid close to the open gate at the courtyard. He hid there, watching as people went in and out through the massive double doors. Somehow he managed to sneak past the guards into the building.

"Mevi-tra is built on a mountain, and inside the massive building are several passageways that lead to other parts. Not sure where to go, Sullivan took the first passageway. The long corridor had crystal rods set several feet apart along its roof that gave a soft light.

"Along the way, Sullivan heard voices and stopped at one of the nooks built along the wall at the bottom. The nook was between two crystal posts in an area the light did not reach. Sullivan could see a man and woman talking as they made their way toward him. He crouched down next to the wall as they passed, unaware of him. When their footsteps had faded behind him, he hurried on. Other hallways branched off, but he went straight until he came to a dead end with four doors. All the doors looked the same–ornately designed in marble stone with the symbols of the solar system.

"Sullivan chose the farthest door to his left and went inside. The room was breathtaking. The walls had beams of gold patterned with velvet blue that came together at the top. The roof reflected the still pool in the middle of the vaulted room, and the pool of water appeared flush with the floor that was like the sky at midnight. Looking at the roof, he could see the reflection of something glowing in the middle of the room.

"Sullivan moved closer to see a glowing orb at the center of the black pool. He moved toward it without thinking, creating a gentle ripple that swept across the pool, which was reflected overhead.

"His curiosity urged him on, even though the celestial feeling in the room made him nervous. He would leave once he had a quick look. The object in the pool was like a piece of the stars and he stared at it, wide-eyed, in amazement. It seemed so close, something just within his reach. So he stretched his hand in to touch it. He was almost there, he thought, so he stretched a little more, but lost his balance and fell into the pool.

"He panicked as fear grabbed him. Flapping his hands, he opened his mouth to scream, but nothing came. He was choked by the water that rushed in, muting his attempt to scream for help.

"He was beginning to lose consciousness as he slipped deeper into the pool. His face was almost even with the glowing orb in the center of the pool when a hand grabbed the back of his shirt and began pulling him back to the surface. Dark clouds gathered around him, and for a few seconds, the only thing he could see was the dream-like brilliance coming from the orb. There was something inside it, he noticed, in the form of a scroll.

"As the light drew away from him, he blacked out. The

figure pulling Sullivan up had not noticed how close he was to the orb until Sullivan's feet brushed it, sending a shock through every part of his being and drawing him out of unconsciousness.

"Sullivan found himself lying on his stomach at the edge of the pool. He took several painful breaths, coughing in between as the water that had ceased his breath emptied. Still fatigued, he turned to see the person that saved him and found his father standing there, soaked through in his blue robe.

"Graham had no anger in his expression or tone, or so it appeared from the outside. He did not act surprised to have found his son far from home, nor did he ask how he got inside the building. He only said, 'You will need to stay here tonight, and Root will get you something dry to wear.'

"A man and woman dressed in white stood at the entrance watching as Graham led Sullivan to the door.

"Sullivan recognized one of them as the person he snuck past. Graham handed Sullivan to Root and stood there for a minute watching as he was escorted to a different room. Sullivan turned once to see his father standing there, watching as he was led away.

"When his son was out of sight, Graham went the opposite way. He entered one of the many rooms inside the temple and locked the door behind him; alone, he let go of his emotions as tears rolled down his cheek.

"Why, why was this happening to him? Graham thought reflectively. He was both angry and sad. If he'd only been there sooner, or had been faster, maybe he would have been able to save him, he thought as he slumped on the only chair in the room in his wet robe.

"When Sullivan was being pulled up, his feet touched the orb, which caused the ring on his father's finger to light up, as well as every Patron around the four Kingdoms. A gathering was planned two weeks from that day, and he knew what was going to happen. His son would be placed in what was known as the marble seal, where he would spend the rest of his life as he began to lose his mind, which was an effect of the scroll, or key of creation.

"The madness is caused by the powerful pull from the other keys of creation guarded by the other Patrons.

"Graham knew that eventually, Sullivan's only obsession would be to obtain the other keys, which would give him untold powers enough to destroy the earth itself, and this was the reason for the creation of the marble seal. Designed to hold anyone consumed by the scroll and in order for the person to be placed in the marble seal, all eight Patrons had to be present. Graham's main concern, outside of his own, was that of his wife. How was he going to break the news?

"Rita was still getting ready when an excited maid burst through the bedroom door. 'Young Sullivan is coming, and with Master Graham.'

"Rita stopped what she was doing and ran out of the room. Graham and Sullivan were some distance away when they saw Rita running toward them. She rushed to Sullivan, picked him up, and kissed him, relieved that he was all right.

"She scolded him as she placed him down. Looking defeated from his mother's rebuke, Graham sent him away and Sullivan ran inside, leaving his mother and father alone. Graham asked Rita to come with him as he turned and started walking away from the house with Rita following. She could see her husband was troubled, as he was quiet and withdrawn.

"She asked where he found Sullivan, breaking the silence a few minutes into their walk. Graham told her, he had followed him all the way to Mevi-tra, but must have gotten lost inside.

"Rita was surprised to hear this. 'This boy someday is going to drive me crazy. Just like you, he's strong-willed, with an insatiable sense of curiosity.' She was trying to lighten Graham's mood, but his flat expression did not change at her attempted tease. Whatever happened must have been bad to set her husband in such a mood. She grabbed his hand to stop him.

"Graham stopped walking and said simply, shaking his

head in regret, 'He fell in...he fell in, and the Council will be gathering in two weeks.' She knew exactly what Graham meant. The shock of his words tore through her. She turned and was about to run away when Graham grabbed her hand and she stopped. Her eyes welled up, and she began to cry as Graham pulled her into an embrace.

"Rita spent that night thinking about what she was going to do. This wasn't going to be her son's fate, she thought as she shifted in bed. Unable to sleep, she quietly rose from bed and tried to tiptoe out of their room, but Graham heard it. He questioned his wife, who tried to act natural, and he went back to sleep.

"What to do? She continued to contemplate as she walked over to Sullivan's room. Rita peeked in and found him curled at the head of his bed, shaking. She hurried over to Sullivan, who was unaware of her presence until she laid her hand on his head.

"'What are you doing here?' he asked, surprised to see his mother in his room.

"'You were sitting curled up at the head of your bed, shaking. Are you okay?'

"'Yes, I'm fine,' Sullivan replied as he pulled up his covers.

"'Are you sure?'

"'Yes, really, I'm fine,' Sullivan replied.

"Convinced, Rita kissed his forehead and as she left the room made her decision.

"The next day, Rita began privately making preparations when Graham was away. When everything was ready, she sent Sullivan away. She knew her husband was bound by his duty as Patron to bring Sullivan in and that she could face disciplinary action for what she was doing, but regardless of the consequence and magnitude of her action, she did it anyway, sending him into hiding with one of her maidservants named Obrie.

"Where they were heading, no one knew, but they were gone for four days and had traveled far into the southern borderland before they were found by the Ackalans that were sent to bring him back. As they escorted the wagon back two days after they were found, something strange happened. The sun was setting that day as Obrie and Sullivan sat inside the wagon when suddenly Sullivan's eyes turned red, then gold, his face slowly becoming translucent. His form also changed, fading into itself like a reflective pool. Obrie screamed, recoiling away as his form drifted toward her. Everyone stopped, and the Ackalans closest to the carriage rushed over, pulling the door open to see a Sullivan wrapped in a rainbow of color suddenly disappear in front of them, leaving Obrie frozen in her seat. That was the last time Sullivan was seen–until now."

A crackly sound came from a snapping twig breaking inside the fire when Iseac stopped speaking. The fire was almost completely died down, with just an orange glow remaining at the base.

Iseac could see the questions in Samuel's eyes as he spoke.

"We have a long day tomorrow; get some rest. There will be time for questions later," Iseac said, as if reading Samuel's thoughts. Sleep was now the last thing on Samuel's mind, with hundreds of additional questions running through it. But as time passed, the soothing touch of sleep came, and he was swept away for the night.

Chapter 17

A Welcomed Surprise

"We have to go," Mosley said, waking Samuel from his sleep. It was still dark out, grayish black from the dew that hovered overhead. For a minute, Samuel wondered why he was woken up in the middle of the night; he could have slept for another hour or two.

"The sun will be rising in another hour, and I would like us to be at the river's edge by noon," Iseac said. Samuel yawned, stretching his arms up to the heavens; he was still tired.

"You can rest on Durack," Iseac said as Samuel was clearing his eyes, "but we have to leave now."

The horses were already saddled and ready to go.

Even as he woke himself up, Samuel thought there was something, not odd, but different about Iseac that he couldn't put his finger on. It started with his companion Mosley, who had a silver ring around his eyes that was even more pronounced at night when he stepped into the firelight.

Two days before, Mosley had run for hours, his endurance unlike anyone he'd ever seen. Iseac himself never appeared tired, even though he was awake before and after Samuel went to sleep; and again, he was already packed and ready to leave. These and other things about Iseac got him thinking–Iseac was more than what he was portraying.

"I would like to walk this time," Samuel said, hoping to use the opportunity to find out more about them as Iseac gave him a quizzical look.

"I would prefer not toppling off while I'm still trying to wake up, if you don't mind," Samuel said flatly, bringing a smile to everyone's face.

"Very well," Iseac said as he tugged on Durack's reins.

They were traveling the back lands of Chartum-Valley that few dared use because of the many sinkholes.

"Have you been to these parts before?" Samuel asked, seeing Iseac's confidence in navigating the land.

"You...could say that," Iseac replied.

"So what are Anamerians?" Samuel asked. "You mentioned them yesterday."

"They are normal beings like you and I, but they are seekers that help bring balance to all things, either in the present or the future."

"Is this the person that can help me find my family?" Samuel asked.

"No, he's not. The person we'll be seeing is called Gabram. He is a Patron from Bremah, which is where we are going."

"I have never been to Bremah before, but I've been to Orie and Bayshia."

"Did your family go to the last harvest festival?" Iseac asked.

"Yes! That is one thing we look forward to doing as a family."

Samuel trailed off. Iseac realized this conversation was only going to lead one way, which was stirring up memories of Samuel's loss, so he cut in, bringing the conversation back to Samuel's original question.

"Bremah, you asked, is about half the size of Bayshia; the only difference is that most of the homes are built from red bricks. However, Gabram, whom we are going to meet, lives outside the city. Patrons like Gabram are overseers—stewards of the scrolls of creation. There are eight of them."

"Where are they located?" Samuel asked.
Iseac looked at him, a faint smile curling the corner of his lip. "They are around the four kingdoms."

"So do the Ackalans of the scroll serve the patron? And is it true that they never sleep, and can they disappear in the dark?" Samuel asked his questions in rapid succession.

Iseac sighed. "Well, why don't you ask one of them."

Mosley, Samuel thought flushing with embarrassment. He was even more surprised to hear Mosley say, "What would you like to know?"

Apparently he had been listening to their conversation, even though he was several feet away from them. Now he was pulling his horse to the opposite side of Samuel, whose embarrassed look made Iseac smile.

He has a youthful innocence, Iseac thought as Samuel tried to hide his embarrassment.

"People exaggerate things, you know," Mosely began. "The ability of the Ackalans comes from their years of training and an awareness of themselves against their surroundings. When the connection is made after a person's mind is unlocked, things that appear extraordinary become ordinary."

Samuel, a few days ago, wouldn't have considered asking such question of an Ackalans, considering it as foolish or even childish. However, after seeing his family disappear in a flame of fire, nothing was outside of the realm of possibility. He wasn't going to presume anything on things he'd once questioned, and it was in this same manner that Mosley responded to this question.

"And no...we can't disappear," Mosley said, "but I can see how someone might believe that. People don't always see what is in front of them because of their preconception. They only see what their eyes tell them should be there."

"Is that what you mean by unlocking the mind?" Samuel asked.

"No, it is more than that. It's something that can't be explained in any way that would make sense to you."

"Why can't it be explained?" Samuel thought, but before he could ask, Iseac cut in on their conversation.

"Hold it," he said, and they turned to look at him.

"We have—" and before he could finish his sentence, an arrow came flying. He didn't have enough time to react, and the force from the arrow pushed him even farther to his right as he tried to move away from it.

It pierced his shoulder just as Mosley rushed in front of him.

Everything happened in a flash. By the time Samuel could react, Mosley had deflected several arrows aimed at them. His hands moved with such speed and grace that Samuel could only stare in awe.

Samuel went pale, then, when he heard the familiar grunting sound that haunted his dreams. It sent a chill down his spine just before they emerged from woods.

The creatures he now knew as Agoras. Behind them, three people on horseback appeared, with their arrows aimed at them.

Gritting his teeth, Iseac pulled the arrow out of his shoulder in a single motion. He turned to Samuel as the spot where the arrow once was began to soak in blood.

"We'll hold them off, but I need you to promise me that you'll go to Bremah and not do anything else."

Samuel nodded his head in response.

"If you want to find your family, he is the only one who can help you. Durack will get you there, and we'll catch up with you later."

Samuel had a flashback, then; remembering that those were the same words his father uttered, and he never came back for them.

"Now go!" Iseac said, cutting in on Samuel's thought. Iseac turned, brushing his hand along Durack's neck.

Samuel knew arguing with Iseac would only get them both killed, and this was not the time, so he reluctantly mounted Durack. Iseac whispered something in his horse's ear. Iseac turned to look at him.

"Hold on," he said just before tapping Durack on its side.

Whatever he said sent the horse galloping with incredible speed, and Samuel had to hold on tight. His surroundings became a blur within minutes as the air rushed past him. The wind muted every other sound except the rhythmic sound of

Durack's smooth gallop. Samuel did not turn his head for fear of what he might see; instead, he leaned forward to protect himself from tree branches as the horse raced through the woods.

Iseac caught a glimpse of Samuel at the of the corner of his eye as he disappeared into the woods with the Agoras encircle them. They were not attacking, but snarled at them as they waved their weapons. Iseac suspected the reason the first arrow didn't kill him was because they wanted him alive. Golans rarely miss.

This was confirmed by the apparent standoff by the Agoras; someone had given the order not to attack. Iseac could see, behind their hunger for blood, the anger and frustration of not being able to act on it.

"Drop your weapons," a voice that sounded like splintering wood said from outside the circle. Iseac was focused on the Agoras, but his eyes drifted up briefly above their heads to see a rider approach. The rider's face was hidden inside the cowl of his cloak and next to him were three other horsemen, their arrows aimed at them.

The arrows were held in place by the unwavering hands of Golans, with their battle colors of red and green splitting their face.

The hooded man dismounted and walked toward Iseac and

Mosley. The Agoras parted as he entered the circle.

"Now," he said, gesturing for them to drop their weapons as he stood in front of them.

"What do you want with us?" Iseac asked as the man pulled his hood off.

The person who stood in front of them was like a corpse that was forced to remain in his body. He was almost as pale as the Agoras, but he had thinning silver hair that was shoulder length, and his eyes were venomous red. He did not respond to Iseac's question, but said instead "Ah...It's been a long time since I've seen your kind." He turned his head slightly to look at Mosley, then returned his gaze to Iseac. "If I give the order, you will be dead, and even the Ackalan can't stop so many of them."

Iseac knew he was right; while he was able to block the pain, he was losing the feeling in his arm. He looked at Mosley, moving his head slightly as he dropped his quarterstaff. Mosley did the same, releasing his weapon and letting it drop to the ground. As he did, the Agoras rushed them to the ground and they were both restrained.

"Tie him with that," the man leading the group said, pointing to Mosley. "They are a lot more dangerous than they appear. Take care of the rider," he said, looking at the Golans, and they rode off after Samuel.

Iseac and Mosley were pulled to their feet and pushed forward as the man lifted his hood over his head again and began walking away.

He stopped after a few steps, turned his head to the side, and said casually, as if talking to himself, "They said to bring you alive, but no one mentioned anything about your companion.

"Take care of him," the man said to the Agora next to him, and he started walking again to his horse. The Agora that was giving the command ran toward the group that was holding Mosley, and he was pulled away. At the same time, Iseac was hit hard in the back. It sent flashes of pain across him, joining the one in his shoulder. He clenched his teeth as he stumbled forward from the force.

"Move it..." the Agora that struck Iseac said, the words foreign to his tongue. They spoke in a strange tongue that Mosley did not recognize or understood as he was led away. While Iseac's hands were tied behind him, Mosley had a wooden log placed over his shoulders so his hands were tied apart.

While most of the Agoras' dominating thoughts had to do with killing humans, their leader was determined not to take any chances with Mosley.

He was about forty yards from Iseac when the leading

Agora kicked him in the back of his leg, bringing Mosley to his knees. He had been studying the small group that was leading him to his execution, and knew this was it as he watched them form a semi-circle around him.

The leading Agora walked to Mosley, his scarred face visible inside his helmet as he stared at him with his deadly blue eyes that held an unknown hatred for humans.

Sunlight glittered off the Agora's jagged blade as he raised his hand to the air. Mosley moved, taking advantage of the split-second opening. He swung the left end of the log that held his hands apart as he rose from his knee. It caught the Agora under his chin, snapping its neck as the force pushed it back. Caught by surprise, it took a second for the other Agoras to react as they rushed forward, determined to end his life.

So he spun the log around, shifting from right to left as best he could with his legs tied closely together, which left him no real room to move. As Mosley fought for his life, he received several cuts to his arm, side, and thigh. An ax was thrown in his direction and he shifted.

It flew past him landing in the forehead of an Agora, who dropped to the ground behind him. The ax handle resting in the forehead of the creature as he glanced at it was an Ackalan. Help had arrived, and in the nick of time.

Just then, other Ackalans appeared. The Agoras around

Mosley became unsure of what to do–continue with their attempt to kill him, attack the approaching Ackalans, or flee.

They chose the latter and began to flee as they were pursued by the Ackalans on horseback.

"Where is Iseac?" Tremay asked while Mosley was still trying to catch his breath.

"He's been taken by a different group not more than forty yards from here—"

Before Mosley could finish his sentence, Tremay was already gone. Several of the Ackalans followed after him, trying to catch up. The soil was damp from morning dew, but they all felt the earth shake as if from a minor tremor. It caused the horses to slow down with fear. Tremay could see, between the trees, what looked like flames with images of people inside them. He jumped off his horse and began to run toward it when the flame disappeared.

"We have to find him," Tremay said as he picked up Iseac's quarterstaff from the ground and moved toward the spot where Iseac would have been standing.

Several of Tremay's companions stood behind him, studying their surroundings. Tremay started walking back when one of his men came up to him.

"We have several of them that are still alive," he said, referring to the Agoras.

"Good," Tremay responded in a tone that held the low current of a tidal wave. "I need some answers," he said under his breath as he made his way to Mosley.

"Join me when you're done," he said to Mosley, who was free of his restraints and attending to his wounds.

Chapter 18

The Mist to Lufgard

The woods were becoming denser the farther in Samuel went. Little rays of light snuck between the trees that seemed to hold the fog in place.

Samuel was holding tightly to Durack's reins as the horse continued to gallop in full stride and with poor visibility. It was hard for Samuel to see where he was heading, and this kept him on edge. He hoped the horse's keen senses would keep them both alive; while his present predicament was at the forefront of his mind, the other part of him still felt guilty for leaving Iseac and Mosley even though he knew he was weaponless, as his quiver was empty of arrows.

"You could do nothing; you would have only been a hindrance," the rational part of him kept saying, but it provided no consolation. Tightening his grip on Durack's reins, Samuel slowed the horse down to a canter, and then to a trot to give himself time to think.

He remembered his promise to Iseac that he would go to Bremah, and if he turned back to help, he would be breaking that promise.

Durack continued to move, slowing some as Samuel

contemplated what to do next. Deep in thought, Samuel did not notice the needle from a piece of broken branch dangling on his trouser just above his right boot. The needle pricked his leg, drawing him out of his musing as he jerked, instinctively bending down to remove the branch. At that instant, he heard three darting sounds in rapid succession on the tree beside him.

He did not have to look at what he knew were clearly the sounds of fired arrows or where they came from. Without thinking, Samuel tugged on Durack's reins, sending the horse into motion. He knew instinctively, even as fear took hold of him, that riding from right to left in a zigzag pattern gave him less chance of been hit, so he held on as tree branches swatted his sides along the way.

Upset at their wasted chance, having been so close, the Golans sat on their horses, watching with their arrows drawn, looking for a better shot. Samuel disappeared into the fog.

One had aimed for his head, the other two his heart. If it wasn't for his sudden move, they would have been done, but now he was on the move again with the fog obscuring their vision.

They sent their horses into motion following after him; soon enough, they would get their shot.

Samuel kept Durack at a gallop while laying low, now that

he knew he was being followed by the same horsemen that had appeared with the Agoras.

"Idiot, did you think they were just going to let you leave?" he said to himself, his cloak tugging his neck as it flapped behind him.

Ignoring the choking sensation, Samuel kept his pace, not wanting to take any chances.

The land sloped down slightly as he rode, his teeth chattering at the hard pace he was going. It wasn't long before he could feel a difference in the air. It was heavier, with the cool breeze of the coast mixed with the smell of fish, smoke, dirt, and an assortment of other things. A few minutes later, he could hear the lively buzz of a busy town. He was getting close. In between the trees, he was soon able to see rooftops, then people moving along a footpath about twenty yards from his clearing. He shifted Durack to his right, staying inside the tree line.

He spotted several old buildings ahead that looked like inns, from what he could see. The fourth building would be the shortest distance from his position.

Samuel burst into the clearing, slowing Durack to a canter halfway from the crowd, and even as the horse was coming to a stop, he dismounted. He barely kept his feet under him as he landed. The momentum sent him into a running motion as he ran into the crowd holding on to Durack's reins.

****

With the fog lifted, the Golans could see better closer to the tree line, and one of them spotted Samuel between the trees. "There," he said, pointing, and they followed in a gallop with their arrows still notched.

The Golans approached the edges of the tree line where Samuel had veered right, still hidden from view. They could see horse tracks from their position that joined the crowd down the slope, but he was gone. They stood there for a minute, looking, before turning their horses around and riding back into the woods.

Even moving within the crowd, Samuel kept looking over his shoulder at the tree line, expecting his assailants to burst out into the open. He saw nothing, but kept searching until his view became obscured by one of the old buildings.

****

Still tense, Samuel looked around as people passed by; after a minute, he decided to look for an inn while trying not to be conspicuous. Until this point, he hadn't given any thought to how he would get to Bremah.

He decided to dig through Iseac's saddlebag and was relieved to find a purse of coin buried underneath a bunch of clothes. Looking around, he chose an inn called the Fishers Bait and made his way in.

The place was packed with travelers from different parts of the world. From the way some of them were dressed, and from what Faray had once told him on one of their trips to Bayshia, these were sailors.

He'd never seen so many gathered in one place, and he was beginning to wonder if the town was a shipping port. Samuel also realized that he was the youngest person in the room. For this early in the morning, the place was reasonably packed, with a few open tables and chairs aged from long use. A young woman was cleaning one of the tables. She had some resemblance to the man behind the bar. His daughter, maybe, Samuel thought.

The slim man behind the bar was past his middle years, with the skin of one who has spent more than a considerable amount of time under the open sky. His eyes were sharp and he had a beak of a nose.

"Welcome to Fishers Bait, young master," the man said in that friendly tone unique to most innkeepers. "What can I get for you?" he asked.

"Something hot...and maybe information," Samuel said almost as an afterthought.

"Leera!" he called to the young woman cleaning a table.

"Could you get our young master here something hot from the kitchen?"

"So what would you like to know?" the innkeeper asked Samuel.

"Do you know of any ships leaving directly for Bremah from this port? Or one heading that way?"

"Well, there aren't really that many that go from Lufgard to Bremah directly; they normally stop at Kadan's Gate first. But..." He paused for a second. "You might be in luck, if what I heard one of *The Night Meadow* crewmen say is true."

The sound of a swinging double door drew the innkeeper's attention for a brief second to the person who was approaching. It was the young woman returning with a tray that held a bowl of soup and flat bread.

The innkeeper returned his attention back to Samuel.

"Where can I find this ship?"

"Oh...yes, just follow the Hallboat Road, you can't miss it. Find the first mate. They are normally the loudest people."

"Thank you," Samuel said, placing four copper coins on the table instead of three.

"I don't charge customers for information."

"I know, but I want to," Samuel said.

"Well, then, I better be returning to my other customers." He swept the coins of the table and left.

Samuel hurriedly finished his soup. It was nice and hot with chunks of fresh fish, but he ate it absentmindedly, his thoughts now set on that ship, even though he was still concerned about the danger out there, which kept him vigilant.

Samuel tried to focus on his bowl of soup, but he continued to scan the tables around him for the eyes he felt were watching him; each time, it was the same. No one was looking.

He took even more caution when he was out of the inn, making sure to stay within or close to other groups heading in the same direction. When he realized he would have no cover on Hallboat Road, he got on Durack and galloped as fast as he could till the ships hidden behind tall oak trees came into view.

He'd never seen such massive structures floating on water before; from his count, there were six of them, with the pier extending far into the river. He dismounted and started walking along the pier looking for the ship known as *The Night Meadow*. The ships were magnificent as he went on each dock, and on the fourth one, he found it.

The ship was made of dark oak with the base painted black; like the others, it was well kept. The wood was so well polished that even with its weathered look, it still had some of its luster. Three massive poles like spires rose from the ship, with massive fabrics rolled up on poles across them.

As Samuel drew closer to the front of the ship, he could hear the voice of a man speaking at the top of his lungs some distance away. The first mate, he thought, as he passed the wooden stairs that led into the ship, guarded by one of the crewmen, who was watching everyone passing by.

"I already have enough dead weight now; pick it up," continued the voice that was now clearer. "Move it, we don't have all day. Be careful with that." The first mate did not cease his endless stream of remarks that the crew took in stride as they moved cargo into the ship. Nothing escaped his gaze, and you could tell looking at the crew that they knew it too.

"How does one secure a place on a ship? " he wondered, unsure of what to do as people walked past him. He stopped an older man with thinning gray hair. He looked local and someone who would know what to do.

"I need a place on this ship," he said, pointing. "Do you know where I can secure a pass?"

"Yes," he said nasally, "you have to talk to that man over there." He pointed to a figure on the dock.

"Thank you," Samuel said just as the man lifted the handle to his cart and walked away with the wheel squeaking behind him.

He was glad to know it wasn't the first mate he had to deal with, until he saw who he was supposed to barter with–he looked even more menacing. But he was determined. He remembered how his father dealt with different traders. Composing himself, he walked over to the man who held the fate of his family.

After the bartering deal was done, Samuel had secured a pass to the ship without losing everything in his purse. He made his way through the crowd by the dock to the ship.

Once cleared, he began making his way up the wooden stairs with Durack, who was skittish even for a well trained horse. As Samuel made his way up the steps, he noticed a well dressed man in fine linen moving through the crowd that parted on his approach. He was accompanied by eight others whose clothes were well cut, but not as fine. A high nobleman, he suspected, as they rode to the first mate.

Seeing the nobleman approaching, the first mate bowed his head in greeting, and the man acknowledged his salute with a wave of his hand.

After a few seconds of watching them talk, the first mate left his post and began to personally escort the Lord with his entourage, who followed behind him.

Samuel and his roommates were settling in when a broad-shouldered crewman walked into their cabin.

"I need all of you out," the crewman said, gesturing to everyone in his view. The man's shirt was partly unbuttoned in the front, with his well-defined muscular arms showing in his sleeveless shirt. No one said anything at first, as everyone began gathering their things.

Samuel, like everyone else, recognized the man immediately; he was the one who had checked his pass before he boarded the ship.

He followed his cabin mates, unsure of what was going on or the reason why they were being moved; the little sense of safety he'd been fostering was beginning to disappear.

"Why?" he thought to himself in despair, wondering if he was ever going to get a break. Nothing seemed to be going his way.

"What is going on?" one of the passengers asked.

"You'll find out soon enough, just watch your head as you step out," the crewman replied.

"Head down, please," the man said once they were outside on the deck, gesturing for them to continue.

Forming a single file, they began making their way down the wooden steps that could admit two at a time. As Samuel approached the steps with several of his cabin mates already down and waiting in a cluster at the dock, he heard the familiar voice of the first mate.

"We only need six, Rex. The rest of them can stay."

Those words did not sink in at first until Samuel saw the

woman in front of him stop midway, turn, and began making her way back up. He was suddenly flooded with relief. Those that were off the ship swarmed the first mate, their voices rising as they gathered around him.

Samuel went back to his small corner of the room, and soon a new group stepped down into the cabin. They were all well dressed and some of them looked around in disgust. These people were part of the group that came in with the wealthy Lord. It all made sense, then; they were the reason why some of the people in his cabin were removed from the ship.

Samuel placed his hands behind his head as he laid back; for the first time in a long time, the knot he felt in his stomach seem to slowly loosen.

After a few minutes of men screaming overhead on opposite sides of the ship, they finally left the docks. He felt the strange sensation of the ship in motion. They were on their way; Samuel took in several deep breaths and closed his eyes, not thinking for once about what lay ahead.

Chapter 19

New Revelation

"We have to find him." Mosley heard Tremay saying as he approached. His commander was staring into the distance, his cloak as still as the man wrapped in it.

"Tracking him will be a little more challenging now...and the Agoras are as useful to us as stone," Tremay said. "I can't let them go, nor do I wish their lives ended."

His commander's deep and level tone carried the strength and power of a man whose physical and mental state was sharper than a razor's edge. Mosley knew he was already formulating a plan even as he spoke.

"There are rumors that they've been attacking small towns and villages, and what I saw here confirms my fear. Whoever commands them is getting bolder, sending them this far for the Anamerian."

Even as Tremay was talking, they heard a snarling sound. It came from one of the Agoras who had regained consciousness, the noise cutting between Tremay's sentences.

They did not turn to see what was going on, ignoring the sound that was a few yards from them, confident that the Agoras would be dead if they made any sudden move or were any threat.

"Since they don't speak in our tongue," Tremay said as if he was never interrupted, "trying to forcefully extract the information from them will achieve nothing. What I need is someone that can retrieve the information directly from their heads. We need to send word to the Patrons, but first I need to know what happened here."

"The Agoras were led by a human," Mosley said, describing their leader as best he could remember. "The man also commanded a team of Golans."

Those words had Tremay turn to face Mosley; there was a quizzical look in his eyes, a little flicker that, for Mosley, spoke volumes, coming from his commander.

"We were heading to Bayshia from Tru'tia when we were drawn by an unusual scene that led us into Chartum-Valley. We found the town's courier dead on the road from arrows that were Golan's. The town, for the most part, was burnt to the ground. Everything in this town–from the buildings, its people, and even their livestock–was destroyed.

"It appeared from the carnage that nothing was spared, but we found an only survivor. A young man named Samuel. Actually," he said, pausing to rephrase the statement, "he found us. During the siege, he and his family found refuge in what used to be a mining tunnel, but they were discovered.

Samuel managed to escape, but his mother and brother were captured.

"Samuel said he saw his family consumed in flames that did not burn the way normal fire did."

It would have been hard to believe until he saw it with his own eyes, Tremay realized. "And how did he describe it?" he asked.

"He said he saw a man create a ball of fire in his hand that expanded till it enveloped everything around the wagon that held his family just before it disappeared. The young man was one of the people we were going to search for in Bayshia, and were surprised to find in Chartum-Valley. The Anamerian promised to help Samuel find his family. Why, I don't know, but first he wanted to get him to a Patron.

"Something about the Anamerian was tied to the boy," Mosley said, as if talking to himself. "I could sense a connection between him and the boy that I cannot explain.

"We were on our way to Kadan's Gate to sail to Bremah when we were ambushed. Iseac sent the boy away on his horse while we held them off, and as soon as we were bound, Golans were sent after him."

Tremay was quiet for a second after Mosley was done speaking.

"We will find this young man you call Samuel, but first

there are growing rumors of things appearing out of the shadows, attacking villages and small towns. If anyone saw these Agoras this far south from the abyss, it will fan the flames of these rumors even more. We need these two alive to extract what we can from them without drawing any attention.

"Here!" Tremay said to Mosley, handing him two small tonic-size containers. Mosley recognized them immediately; the tonic would knock both Agoras out in a matter of minutes once it touched their tongues.

"I'm not sure how well this will work on them," Tremay said, "since they aren't human, but we'll find out soon enough."

Minutes later, Mosley returned.

"It is done," he said. Tremay raised his right arm over his head, twirling his forefinger in the air, and the Ackalans all mounted their horses.

Mosley called out, whistling, and soon his horse appeared out of the woods, trotting toward him. As his horse was approaching, Mosley took several quick steps and leaped into the air to settle on his horse's saddle.

The captured Agoras that were now unconscious were tossed at the front of the Ackalans' horses, their bodies covered so as not to be seen.

Tremay and the Ackalans trotted into the woods under the

quiet sound of their horses' hooves, which was muffled by wet leaves.

They soon discovered the track of the three Golans and a fourth one that could only be Samuel's. While Mosley's demeanor, like every true Ackalan, was unreadable, he hoped Samuel's luck was still holding.

They had to be quick and vigilant at the same time, knowing that Golans were extraordinarily great marksmen, even as they followed Samuel's tracks. They saw no indication from the tracks that they had caught up to him, but that didn't mean much, since they didn't necessarily have to catch up to him. The Golans' intent wasn't to capture but to end the life of their intended victim.

The wooded area soon opened up to a little fishing town about half a mile way. The street from their vantage point was busy with people moving about and traders trying to sell or buy goods from people that came inland.

From what Tremay could tell, Samuel's tracks indicated that he made it into the town and that he wasn't followed past the tree line. The Golans' tracks veered left back into the woods; either they got their target or decided to end their pursuit. Whatever the reason, they would find out soon enough.

"As you all know," Tremay said, "the sun will be setting in

a few more hours, and we know someone out there saw Samuel. We have an hour to confirm his presence here and what he decided to do. We will meet north of this position just past the watch post."

Tremay chose the watche's post for two reasons. First, the road by the post was the way to Kadan's Gate; if they were to discover that Samuel had moved on, they would already be heading that way. Second, and more important, Tremay wanted to make sure no one saw what they were carrying, as the Agoras were not always completely covered.

Tremay chose four men within the group and asked that they remove all items that would identify them as Ackalans.

While they were doing this, Mosley gave a clear description of Samuel–how he looked and what he was wearing. Once the men were ready, they rode out one at a time into Lufgard, spacing themselves so no association could be made.

Within the hour, the four men returned. After reviewing the information they'd gathered from the street and inns, it was clear, or at least every indication showed, that Samuel had escaped his assailants.

An innkeeper claimed to have helped him and said that he may have boarded a ship called *The Night Meadow* to Bremah, even though most of the ships were heading to Kadan's Gate; rarely do ships go straight to Bremah from Lufgard.

"Fortune must smile on this Samuel," Tremay thought just before saying, "We'll send a message to the Patron in Bremah before leaving Kadan's gate."

The sun was past its zenith when they mounted their horses again; with the signal from Hildra, Tremay's second in command, they headed back into the woods, away from the main roads heading to Kadan's Gate.

As they rode off, Tremay pulled his horse next to Mosley. "Let's hope the young man's fortune is as steady as the northern star. His importance to the Anamerian makes him important us." With that, he rode off to the head of their group.

Chapter 20

Memories and Letting Go

Samuel's first day on the ship was a blur as exhaustion dragged him to sleep. He was met on the other side by nightmares, the horror from recent events playing in his dreams. Startled awake by this terror, he was left both physically and mentally drained.

The weather the second day was rougher as thunderstorms pounded the ship with heavy waves. The violent undulation made Samuel queasy, and he threw up once.

"Take this," one of his cabin mates said, seeing Samuel's flushed look. "It is an illacium leaf; it will help soothe your stomach and stop your heaving."

Samuel raised his head to look at the young woman. "Thank you," he replied as he took the cup she was handing him.

The swaying motion did not cease throughout the day, but went on into the night. The next morning the sea was calm, as if the night before never happened; the sky was clear blue like the water itself, with the breeze of the Kadan River driving them along.

Samuel stepped outside his cabin for the first time and was

amazed at how vast the river was; there was no land in sight as far as his eyes could see. How the sailors knew where they were heading was a mystery to him.

Looking around, he found a spot on the deck close to the foremast. It was a little nook with somewhat of a view. He walked over to the corner of the ship and sat down watching as others came out from their cabins to enjoy the weather. It was nice being out in the open, even though the sun provided little warmth.

A few days ago, Samuel's thoughts had been about finding his family and then trying to escape the Golans that were seeking his life. It had never crossed his mind until now how he would find Gabram in a city almost as vast as Bayshia.

He hoped that people weren't as ignorant as he was and that in a big city like Bremah, someone would know where he could find the Ackalans and they would be able to lead him in the right direction.

As Samuel sat wrestling with his thoughts, he noticed a lump in his trouser pocket. He dipped his hand in and pulled out the object. He'd forgotten about the necklace with the emerald ring that he had picked up in Bayshia.

Maybe the Patron would have an explanation for what happened to him in Bayshia. Or would he think he was crazy? It wasn't any crazier than everything else that had happened to him. He remembered Iseac didn't think he was crazy when he mentioned people disappearing in flames. This wasn't anymore crazy than that. Thinking of Iseac, how was he going to break the news of his capture to Gabram? He wasn't sure of their relationship and how close Gabram was to Iseac. He would wait and see what happened, and then determine the best approach.

The sail the rest of the way wasn't as rough as the second day; however, Samuel couldn't wait to be on solid ground again. Every day looked the same, as if they weren't moving, but on the sixth day, the man in the crow's nest sounded the alarm.

"Land in sight!" he cried. "Bremah ahead!"

Samuel looked up to at the watcher standing high on the foremast, his words ringing out like a tower bell. Those words sent the crew into motion as they dashed across the deck. The men rushed about their duties, preparing to dock, with the first mate driving the crew to quicken their pace. Somehow, in what looked like chaos, they knew exactly what to do.

For the first time, Samuel saw the mountainside over the horizon. He squinted; making sure his eyes weren't playing tricks on him. He could not believe he made it, as the ship moved closer to land, and then the tip of a massive wall slowly appeared out of the horizon. It was soon obscured by trees as they got closer to docking.

It was past midday when they docked and Durack, like Samuel, couldn't wait to be off the ship. The horse was skittish, urging Samuel on as they made their way down the wooden steps of the ship.

The place was different and one could not miss the reddish stone used in the construction of the stores that lined the street by the harbor. It reminded Samuel of an ant mound.

The streets were lined with long rows of shops that looked the same at a glance, with the only distinguishing feature being their hanging metal signs that dangled overhead. A few shops had their signs mounted directly on the wall.

The streets were paved close to the harbor. As Samuel stood looking around at the busy street, he felt an odd sensation that had nothing do with the humidity or the fishy smell that was mixed with the crowd. He knew he wasn't moving, but he felt as if he were still in motion. It felt so strange that he had to look down at his feet just to make sure he wasn't moving.

"We better get going, then," Samuel said to Durack as he held the horse's reins. The last time he remembered seeing so many people was at the harvest festival.

A little intimidated, having never traveled unaccompanied by a family member, Samuel took a deep breath before making his way through the crowd. Hawkers moved about with their goods balanced on their heads. They seemed to concentrate on the new influx of people, with Samuel's ship being one of the new arrivals.

He pressed on through the crowd, looking at the different establishments and the people that passed by, some with strange contraptions that went over their shoulders allowing them to balance their goods in front.

Samuel decided he would find an inn inside the city, wherever that was, once he was away from the harbor; but first he needed to get directions. His first stop was at the tavern called the Ram Rode, and he was surprised to see the place filled with people. Apparently taverns here at the coastal area of Bremah were just as busy during the day as one would expect at night.

He could not believe what the server girls were wearing—sleeveless and low-cut dresses that extended just above their knee. No wonder the place drew so many male customers, like bees to honey. It wasn't any different at the Lady's Fisher, which was close, but on the opposite side of the street.

"It makes sense," Samuel thought, as both taverns were competing for the same customers.

After a few minutes of waiting to be served, Samuel decided to keep going. Hopefully there will be others ahead that aren't as busy as these two, he thought as he moved on.

Samuel quickly realized that the farther up he went, the more spread out the shops became, so when he saw the next tavern, he decided not to try his luck on a fourth. Even as he approached, the place looked less crowded.

As he was making his way across the road to the tavern, he saw two uniformed patrol guards on horseback. They scanned the street for any signs of trouble as their horses moved gently along.

"Why didn't I think of this," he thought. "They will know how I can get to the city." As Samuel picked up his pace to catch up with the uniformed men, he heard his name. It was clear, as if the person were standing next to him. He stopped and turned to see who it was that had called. In the middle of the street, a man dressed in a silk blue robe stood, looking at him. At the sight of the stranger, everything else faded, making him appear alone. Samuel blinked, taken by what just happened, as things returned to normal.

The man's clothing was no longer the blue robe he thought he saw, but something different. He was now wearing a white woolen shirt and brown riding trousers, but he was still in the same spot as before. The stranger gestured for him to come even as he made his way over to him.

"I am Gabram," the man said, bowing his head in a nod. "I

have been expecting you. Please follow me!" He turned and started walking back into the crowd.

It took a minute for Samuel, who was still marveling at what just happened, to realize that Gabram was leaving. He picked up his pace to catch up to him.

"I must be going crazy," Samuel muttered under his breath. Whatever was happening to him, he did not like it. He hoped all of this would go away once he found his family and returned home.

He focused on staying with Gabram, who moved through the crowd like water between trees. They soon took a side street away from most of the crowd and stopped at a single building with a woman tending to the shrub in front.

"Can you ride?" Gabram asked, and Samuel nodded in response.

"Good. Wait here for me." Gabram walked into the building. Samuel watched the woman, who was past her middle years, clear the area around the purple and white flowered shrub. When Gabram returned, appearing from the side of the building, he was on horseback; with him were two men dressed in clothing similar to what he remembered Mosley wearing. Ackalans, he thought, relieved that he had made it.

"They are here for your protection," Gabram said. "We

have much to talk about, but right now we have a long ride ahead of us."

Gabram watched Samuel get on Durack before sending his horse into a trot, riding between the waiting Ackalans. He picked up his pace to catch up with Gabram and they rode off with the harbor slowly fading behind them.

They rode in through a massive gate known as the western entrance. A notable number of armed guards were watching as people passed by. Gabram led them north around the city with Samuel watching in amazement at how different Bremah was. Most of the streets were paved with the same reddish cobblestones as the harbor, and some of the buildings were made of the same material, too. In areas where buildings weren't obscured by trees, he could see long stretches of homes built together, which he'd never seen before.

It was past midday when they arrived at the northern gate, which was not as heavily guarded. It led out of the city into the open plain.

The sun was below the horizon, and they followed a natural path created through the trees when Samuel smelled it: burning wood from a chimney. "We are getting close to homes again," he thought, just as what looked like a cottage appeared overhead between the trees. From a distance, the windows on the building were like the glowing eyes of an owl.

They rode down a steady slope toward the only house in the middle of the woods and unsaddled their horses in a fenced area by the house. They made their way to the front door, led by Gabram.

Inside, they were greeted by Gabram's wife; as soon as she saw that they had guest, she went straight to work.

"Let me get this child something to eat," she said as she scurried off into the kitchen.

"Maria, your father is home," she called out, and a young girl in her teens ran out to meet Gabram. Maria was dressed in a long purple square-neck gown with a white short-sleeved shirt underneath. Her hair was pulled back, held in place by a white ribbon. She ran into Gabram's arms and gave him a hug as he kissed her on the forehead.

Once Maria took her head from her father's shoulder, Gabram gestured toward Samuel.

"I would like you to meet a friend of mine. Samuel, this is my daughter, Maria."

"Nice to meet you," Samuel said, bowing his head slightly.

She smiled in return. "Nice to meet you, too."

"Samuel will be staying with us for a while. Do you mind taking his things to the vacant room? And let your mother know we have two more guests outside."

"Yes, Father," she said before disappearing with Samuel's

saddlebag.

Sometime later, they all sat at the table as supper was served. Gabram's wife was a stout woman with shoulder-length hair and an average build. The table was covered with food by the time she sat next her husband.

"Please, go ahead," Gabram said as he began to serve himself. While Gabram's wife took small bites, she scanned everyone's plate and cup, ensuring that none was empty. Samuel declined more after his second serving, but took her offer of a bucket of hot water and a washcloth for the morning.

"Samuel," Gabram announced, "is going to be staying with us a while and he'll be working with me."

"Where are you from?" Maria asked

"Chartum-Valley," Samuel replied, and Gabram's wife looked up at him, not sure if what she heard was correct.

"Is that the same valley north of Orie?" she asked with some surprise in her tone.

"Yes!"

"That is a long way from home," she said just before Maria cut in again. "Tell me about this Chartum-Valley?"

"Maybe some other time," Gabram chimed in. "Let him eat his food." Gabram changed the subject to other small matters, such as things going on in the city and at home. When they were done with supper, Maria was asked to show him to his room.

Samuel's room was lit by two oil lamps, one on the wall next to the door and the other on the only table in the room. A single bed was pushed close to the far wall, with a chair tucked underneath the table with the second lamp. To the right of the table, which was at the base of his bed, was an oak dresser four feet tall.

Alone in the room, tired from the day's travel, Samuel lay on the bed with his hands behind his head, staring at the roof, his thoughts distant. The short time he'd spent with Gabram made him realize how much he missed his family, with everyone sitting at the table for supper after a long day at the farm. The aroma of his mother's cooking and the long nights talking and playing with his brothers seemed like such a long time ago.

The feeling of loss ran through Samuel's mind in waves, stirring his emotions. Like a rock on a sheet of ice too weak to hold its weight, Samuel's eyes began to swell with tears. He broke down and weep till sleep came and took him.

When Samuel woke up the next day, he found a note underneath his door.

Opening it, it read, 'You'll find a washcloth with a bucket of hot water and some clean clothes by your door. What you are wearing will be cleaned by the time we return.'

"I hope they fit," Gabram said when Samuel came out of his room. He remembered Iseac once wearing this shirt while he was preparing him for his unlocking not that many years ago.

"Yes, they fit just fine, thank you," Samuel said.

He was dressed in black trousers and a deep green shirt laced in front and embroidered vertically with a gold pattern along the left side. It was a nice shirt, or, at least, nicer than anything he'd ever owned.

"Walk with me," Gabram said as he handed Samuel what looked like a new cloak, and they made their way into the misty morning.

A single leaf dropped from one of the trees; it swayed in the air as they passed by. A new season was about to begin.

Chapter 21

A Hole to the Abyss

Iseac heard a growling sound as he was jabbed from behind; his vision was still spotty, but he blindly stepped forward, not wanting to be pushed again. As he walked, he couldn't help but notice the rancid smell that clung in the air that made it hard for him to breathe. He felt as if he was being choked and coughed, trying not to breathe in the foul smell. He was pushed again and asked to pick up his pace.

Along the way, his vision came into full focus and he could see they were somewhere underground, or in a cave, maybe; he wasn't sure.

The tunnel he was in was narrow and could only admit four normal-sized adults at a time. The walls had red gems planted along a rough surface that gave off a soft glow and they were the only sources of light along their way. The tunnel in some spots branched off to unknown areas, with each junction supported by heavy wooden beams.

Outside of the low grunts and stomping sound of footsteps behind and in front of him, Iseac heard another sound. It was a low murmur that grew the farther in they went, and after a short span, was clearly. It was the crackling sound of whips mixed with screams and the clanking sound of working tools. The sound of raised voices that weren't human giving commands rose and fell along the way.

As they meandered through the tunnel, they came to a vast opening inside the cave. Several yards from their position was a suspension bridge. As they crossed the massive canyon, Iseac saw other bridges above and below him as far as the eye could see.

"How long has this been going on?" he wondered as they moved across.

Once he was over the bridge, they led him through a wider tunnel that sloped down slightly. Just before it leveled off, the Agoras in front of him stopped.

From where he was standing, he saw two armed men with their backs facing him. Guards, he suspected. They were abnormally broad and muscular, with networks of veins making their way up their necks. The guards' breastplates were dull and dark, like the cave, and their helmets looked like they were built right on their massive heads.

One of them turned to look at Iseac and he was surprised to see a wolfish face. They were half beasts with yellow eyes and thin pupils. The creatures all had a grayish tone to their skin, with arms wide as a bull's hind legs.

This part of the tunnel, Iseac observed, was darker, and

instead of gems, they had fire posts.

The man who led the group spoke to the two guards briefly and then left with his men, leaving Iseac alone with the guards.

"Bring him," the one in charge said, and Iseac moved before he was pushed. In the dim light he saw bars lining this section of the tunnel. There hadn't been any along the way till now. This was one of the areas where the people were being held. The guard in charge opened one of the iron gates and before Iseac could step in, he was pushed inside. Iseac fell, sliding on the dirt floor as the rusty cage was locked behind him.

He rose from the floor, listened to the sound of the guards walking away until he couldn't hear them anymore. He had no light in his cell as he pushed himself up and grunted from applying weight on his bad arm. He felt stiff all over. A result, he suspected, was due to the way they had traveled to this place. He made himself walk to his cell bars. Fire posts were placed on both sides of his cell, both dim, so he couldn't see much, but at least he knew the guards were a safe distance away.

Iseac took in a deep breath, allowing his weariness to overcome him as he got down on one knee. He placed his left hand on the damp floor and began to concentrate.

It was hard to focus with all the pain. It felt as if every part of his body was pounded back together. His head was still foggy from the loss of blood, but after several minutes of painstaking concentration, images of his four walls came into view. He began the slow process of spreading his mind and, within seconds, flashes of life began to pop up around him, but he was too exhausted to continue, so he withdrew.

Yosterio was a lot of work, and he needed to conserve his energy till he found out why he was being held. He had his suspicions.

After weeks of mining and watching people fight for food that was delivered once a day, time became subjective. Iseac, like the others, looked forward to the gathering. It was an arena, of a sort, where he and roughly five hundred other people were herded. In this cramped space, some struggled for the best position, with everyone looking up for what was coming. A black metal pot containing food enough to feed fifty was poured down into the area. They did this throughout the day because of the number of people the area could hold. Those who could not fight died from starvation, while others were killed by those stronger in the fight for food, with the guards watching above.

"You there," the grinding bass of one of the guards called

to Iseac as he stepped toward his cell, unlocking it. It had been a long time since anyone had paid him any attention; he was beginning to wonder if he was just another victim.

"Around your neck," the guard said, tossing Iseac a metal chain with an open ring at the end.

He looked up into the wolfish yellow eyes of the guard, whose size was almost the weight of his cell, and without saying a word, Iseac rose up, walked over to the chain, and clamped it around his neck. The creature spoke to Iseac with the same distaste it had for all humans.

"While my men enjoy the chase and killing those of your kind that think they can escape because they have not been bound...this, I guess, helps to tame that urge," He watched Iseac pick up the chain.

"Good," he said as if addressing an animal, once he heard the clasping sound of the ring around Iseac's neck. He tugged on it, jostling Iseac forward before he was led out of his cage.

The creature took him through a different part of the tunnels. For several minutes they made their way in almost pitch blackness with the guard, who could clearly see in the dark, leading the way.

After several minutes, a flickering light appeared overhead. As they got closer, the tunnel opened up, revealing the first double doors he'd ever seen inside the cave. Two guards stood at the entrance. They relaxed, lowering their weapons when they saw their commander.

They let them through, closing the door behind them. Once inside, they made their way through several open draperies that extended from the rooftop of the long hallway. This part of wherever they were was completely different from the damp rock wall he was used to seeing.

Finally, he thought. He was going to meet the person behind all the people that have been disappearing.

Ahead of them were several young women standing along the side of archway they were approaching. They were scantily dressed, but clean, and stood evenly split on opposite sides of the wall, watching something in the direction they were heading.

They turned briefly to look at them and just as quickly returned their attention to what they were looking at before.

The men facing the entrance as they entered lifted their heads to look at them; but they weren't the ones who caught Iseac's attention. His eyes were instantly drawn to the figure who had his back turned to him, dressed in a dark red silk robe similar to a Patron.

The man took his hands from the table as he stood straight. Iseac could not help noticing his companions watching as he turned. The man had a narrow face with dark blond hair. His feet made no sound as he walked down several flights of a well-polished marble tile to meet them.

He was of average build and taller than Iseac, standing at the same level. His hair was cut below his ears and eyes ashen gray as he looked at Iseac as if studying a piece of his missing puzzle. He half-raised an arm and opened his fingers in a flickering motion. The chain around Iseac's neck snapped and dropped to the ground.

"Thank you, commander; I will take care of this one," he said, dismissing the creature. He walked around Iseac once before speaking.

"We know who you are, Anamerian. Do you see the wreath boy?" he asked rhetorically.

"Your gift," he said with some distaste, "is what our Lord seeks. If you do as you are told and prove yourself worthy of his mercy, then maybe your FALLING will not be cut short.

"Tomorrow we shall begin, and you do not want to find out what will happen if your information is false," he said, picking up his slow and purposeful walk again around Iseac.

"My companions think we should do it without you, but they will need parts." The man sounded as if he hadn't quite made up his mind.

"As tempting as that sounds, I've asked that we hold off for now and give you a chance, with the right incentive. Young men nowadays need something to help them stay focused, right?"

The man stopped pacing and looked at Iseac. "I wonder what yours might be."

He raised his hand in the air, beckoning at someone Iseac could not see. A guard came out from the corner of the room with someone held tightly in his right arm. Iseac hoped it wasn't whom he suspected it was. As the person came to view, anger flared inside him. It took a considerable amount of effort not to lash out at the guard and everyone in the room.

It took a second, but he recognized the person. Elena. Her hair was matted in dirt. There were bruises on her arms and legs, which was also covered in dirt. Her upper arm was like a twig wrapped around the guard's massive hand. She lifted her head to look at him and dropped it back down as the men in the room watched him for some reaction.

"It appears," the man in the red robe said, "the Anamerian does not know this woman. Maybe I was mistaken. I guess she is as useless to him as she is to me."

He reached toward her, straightening his arm as if trying to reach out and slowly clenching his fingers. Elena grabbed her neck and began to struggle violently, trying to pull apart an invisible noose around her neck. Her face slowly turned red.

"Stop," Iseac croaked, as if the words were ripped out of

his mouth. The man in red turned to look at him.

"Oh, so she does mean something to you," he said dispassionately.

"Don't hurt her," Iseac said, conceding to his test.

"Good. I'm glad we have an understanding." He relaxed his fingers and Elena dropped to the ground, coughing. "Take her away," he said, waving his finger. Taking their cue, two of the women ran up to him.

"Show him to his quarters," the man said as he started making his way back up to join his companions.

It had never crossed his mind, but now, seeing Elena, Iseac feared the worst for his family and townspeople.

"Follow me," the servant said, breaking his thoughts.

He glanced at the man in the red robe before following the young woman through a different doorway. He stayed with the young woman as she scurried along, fading in and out of the firelight on their way, until they arrived at a section of the tunnel with a red stone that provided the only light in the area. The soft glow revealed a door made of stone.

It was several inches thick and two guards stood waiting, their massive eyes bright in the dim light.

"Here," the servant said, standing next to the door that was open.

Iseac said nothing as he walked past her into the room.

Once inside, the massive door was pushed in until it closed. The clacking sound of keys followed as the door was locked behind him.

His cell was whitewashed, so even though there was no light, he could still see a little. Oddly enough, Iseac was relieved to find the place not as damp. His cell was empty except for a tin bucket, bowl, and cup. The cup reminded Iseac that his throat was dry. He reached for it and discovered it empty. Disappointed, he sat down, crossing his legs.

After all that had just happened, he was beginning to reconsider his original plan, which was to wait for Samuel and the Ackalans while he gathered information on their enemies' plans; but now that Elena was here–and maybe his family–he needed to do something.

He was beginning to formulate a new plan when a tray came sliding toward him. It stopped halfway in his direction, and he rushed over to pick it up. He saw scraps of meat in some sort of broth that had spilled some along the way.

He dug in, eating with the fierce intensity of a wild animal.

Within minutes it was all gone, but his stomach growled for more. When the tray was clean, he placed it back down and stared at his right hand, opening and closing his fingers. He was pleased to see that his arm was getting better every day.

His shoulder was still sore and stiff, but there was no

permanent damage. He took a look at his shoulder, now that he could see better than before; the area where the arrow struck was still covered in dry blood, now mixed with dirt. He unbuttoned his shirt to examine the area and was pleased to see that it was beginning to heal.

After a considerable amount of time contemplating the next plan of action, Iseac made his decision; he placed his right hand on the floor and concentrated. Soon he gained sight outside his cell.

The numbers of tunnels from his chamber were so numerous that he could not make sense of the maze. There were twice as many people on this side than those in the cell where he was initially held. It made things difficult, but he would search every day until he found her, using the necklace that he saw she was still wearing.

While yosterio allowed him to brush through and see images of a vast number of people, focusing on a single object took more effort. After a short time, Iseac withdrew from exhaustion.

He could sense the guard's presence the next day before he heard the clacking sound of a key unlocking his door.

"They are waiting," the guard said, tossing him the familiar chain to fasten around his neck. "Now it begins," Iseac thought as he walked over to the chain.

Chapter 22

History Behind the Story

Samuel kept up with Gabram as they made their way through the woods that led them in a semi-circle to the back of Gabram's house, from what he could see. They were now on a footpath that gently sloped up as they walked side by side.

"Something is coming...worse than the great battle at Ambacer..." Gabram said, turning his head sideways to look at Samuel, "and you are a witness of this brewing storm."

The battle of Ambacer, Samuel thought. He remembered listening to the tale told long ago of that battle at the valley of Ambacer, where Orums (giant half men) and other beasts never before seen fought against men.

The story was of a man named Rorrah, a former mercenary who rose in his king's service and, over time, began handling matters the king wanted dealt with privately, outside his Council. Those who served with Rorrah respected him and trusted him with their lives.

Over time, Rorrah won the heart of the king's only daughter, Sarah, and so became the first king not of royal blood. For fifteen years, King Rorrah plotted to expand his role. Rorrah was said to be an attractive man, with both physical strength and the cunning tongue of a great speaker. Building a correlation with outlanders, including the Orums and creatures never before seen by men, he invaded the lands north, destroying those that did not swear fealty to him, including the king.

As rumors of his invasion north reached the kings from the other Kingdoms, they sent spies to corroborate the information and learned that it was true. They sent messages to meet with Rorrah, which he declined.

Rorrah's intention for the kings was clear; they needed to be prepared to defend their Kingdoms, so they began making preparations for war, knowing they could be next.

Rorrah's army continued to grow as he swept the northern lands. It was said that his men were so numerous there were ten for every person in Bayshia during the harvest festival.

Rorrah's men moved west and were met by King Leeram. For two days they fought unceasing, and by the third day, Leeram knew they would all die there. So as the sun rose the following morning and the commanders prepared for their final stands, they heard the royal horns of the southern Kingdom. There was silence, at first as the men of Leeram stared in the direction of the sound. Then they heard it. The low thundering stomp of horses as they appeared out of the horizon, dressed in the royal colors of red and gold, with the banner of the rising sun flapping in the air. The men of Leeram raised their voices in a thunderous hail as King Henric rode in with the sun rising behind him.

The rousing cheer was reported to have been heard by Rorrah's men, who were surprised to hear that men from the south had come to fight alongside the army of Leeram, which had never been done before. The surprise, however, did not deter the men of Rorrah, who were on the attack; by the end of the third day, they had both lost almost equal amounts of men.

Something did changed on the third day, as the men of Rorrah were beginning to lose heart. They hadn't planned for such a long siege.

Sensing victory, both kings decided to take the offensive on the fourth day. But Rorrah's men held their ground, and that night, men from the east rode in to aid King Leeram of the west. With the reinforcements, they scattered and drove back Rorrah's troops.

It took two years after that victory for most of the land north to be reclaimed. Rorrah was killed in the battlefield and the outlanders were pushed back to what is now known as the "Abyss of Rorrah." It was the bloodiest war ever recorded in history, caused by a single man who tried to bring the four Kingdoms under one rule.

"One of the things very few people know about the battle

at Ambacer," Gabram said "is why the rulers of the south and east came to the aid of the king in the west. In those days, it was not known for a king to leave his Kingdom to aid another in a war that wasn't his own.

"The story does not tell of the true hero behind the victory: an Anamerian called Ryzin. He told the kings where the battle was and why their Kingdoms needed to be involved, breaking the old tradition of kings defending just their own land without assistance, because of the age-old saying that a king is not fit to rule if he cannot protect his own Kingdom.

"Iseac is the Anamerian," Gabram said, trying to help Samuel understand the magnitude of what he was going to tell him next, "and like those before him, his purpose was to find you.

"Two others are like you, and there is someone who knows that the three of you will be a danger to him and his plans, if each of you comes to know your true self."

Samuel remembered Mosley saying something about a person knowing his true self. Now it makes sense. "No wonder I felt something different about him...a connection, even."

"But why me?" Samuel asked. "I'm the son of a farmer and no threat to anyone."

"We are all more than we appear. We only allow the things around us to define what we become."

"I don't understand."

"Have you had something happen to you, or done something you could not explain?" Gabram asked.

"Yes," Samuel replied.

"Those things you can't explain are instances when our mind brushes against the fabric of our true self."

Samuel remembered then what happened to him in Chartum-Valley. He had seen Iseac's face in his mind before he met him, and Gabram's transformation in the middle of the street.

"I'm sure you've already figured it out, but the people who are holding your family cannot be defeated by mere strength of arms. You are important; they destroyed your town just to find you, and Iseac sent you to me to find out what you are. I hope you are ready for what I'm going to show you."

"How did Gabram know my town was destroyed and because of me?" he thought. It couldn't be true.

"You are more of a threat to this being than you think, and he will stop at nothing until you and the others are dead," Gabram said. "For now, think of our time as a respite from what lies ahead and focus your thoughts on what you will be learning."

They walked through the trees along a steady slope that opened up into a patchy meadow. The landscape slowly changed along the way until only rocks could be seen, as they were close to the base of a mountain.

Samuel followed Gabram along a path that only he could see as they made the steady climb up. They stopped at an open area on the mountainside; it had taken them all of that morning.

On their way to the top, it was becoming harder to breathe. Samuel had to take deeper breaths that even then did not seem to be enough.

"The air is thinner because of how high we've come," Gabram said, noticing the color on Samuel's face. "It takes getting used to, but your body will adjust soon enough."

Standing in an alcove high on the mountain, Samuel looked over the trees at the vast landscape. On the south side was the magnificent city of Bremah, with its great wall and reddish buildings that looked like an ant mound in the distance.

"This place frees the mind from things that hold it down there," Gabram said, referring to what Samuel was looking at. "Come...sit!" When Samuel was seated, he tossed him a water skin. Gabram appeared unruffled from their hike, from what Samuel could see as he drank.

"I know you may feel, so far, that circumstances have directed your path, leaving you with no choice," Gabram said.

"But right now I want you to know that you do have a choice. You can take this opportunity to rebuild a new life for yourself here in Bremah, or I can help prepare you for what is known as the 'unlocking.' It will change your life permanently and give you power in return. You will be anew, unbound by the memories of your old life.

"Think on it and let me know what you choose," he said before going to sit at the ledge, staring into the distance. Samuel sat there deep in thought, remembering the aroma from his mother's kitchen, his father walking in from the fields with his older brother, Faray. He'd always looked up to Faray and still remembered the day he was given his first bow. He remembered how he and Elye got into trouble tying a burning branch to Miss Reonna's hog, their running in the woods by the lake, and many other memories he cherished. "What wouldn't I be willing to sacrifice for my family," he thought, knowing that they could already be dead.

The sun rested on the horizon when Samuel walked over to Gabram. He had made his decision.

"I will do anything for my family," he said in a tone that left no doubt, "and will stop at nothing to find them."

"Good," Gabram said, pleased with his decision. "Lowman will work on getting you physically ready, and he will be waiting for you in the morning."

Gabram began his instructions as the sun slowly slip below the horizon.

"The mind is like a spider's web, and everyone's web is different. At the core of each web is what is known as your true self. Accessing the core brings back locked knowledge and abilities long forgotten. It allows you to see beyond regular sight–you may hear and even understand the language of the earth and many other things hidden from men. A few know how to command the elements. Once the core is awakened, it cannot be changed; and for a person not fully prepared, it could drive them to madness or even kill them. This is the choice we all have to make.

"Now, there are three things you need to know and remember before we begin. First, everything around us is alive and connected. Second, and this lends itself to the first, every living thing has knowledge in its own sphere. This means you can seek or use their help; an example of this was when I called you at the port. I had my call whispered in your ear by the wind."

Samuel remembered the feeling, hearing Gabram whisper in his ears several yards away.

"The third and final thing you need to understand about the unlocking," Gabram said, his tone emphasizing its importance, "is this process does not only awaken things in your mind, but it also, over time, severs ties to things and people you love. This process can be accelerated by how much you use this gift."

Gabram paused to let the information sink in before continuing with his instruction. This, you could say, was the beginning or the turning point in what would become Samuel's new life.

They arrived back at the cottage later that evening. Samuel was exhausted both mentally and physically, and he fell into bed without remembering to disrobe.

Chapter 23

The Awakening

Samuel was woken up before sunrise the next morning by Gabram, who didn't say how early his meeting with Lowman was going to be.

Still exhausted from the night before, Samuel dragged himself out of bed, got dressed, and made his way to meet Lowman, a man of average build with narrow eyes and jet-black hair tied in a knot behind his head. After several painful mistakes, it didn't take long for Samuel to become more alert, as Lowman showed him different self-defense techniques, including proper posturing and motion. He showed Samuel the proper way to cover a blind spot and how to use an opponent's strength to his advantage.

"Remember, flow with their force and let their strength become your energy," he reminded Samuel again and again in his instructions.

Samuel learned about the different pressure points in the human body and how to balance properly on a horse with a weapon, while Gabram instructed him, in between his physical training, on the current rulers of the four Kingdoms and their various customs.

In addition to all this, Samuel was instructed on the different Patrons that would be gathering soon to meet him and what each would contribute to the process of connecting the web that would reveal his true self.

He spent long hours learning and practicing how to survive different terrains using only material that would be available in each setting. Lowman taught him the tricks to hiding in almost plain sight and how to quickly set up a trap and create a deadly weapon. He learned how the wind affects velocity and the proper positioning of one's self, on and off a horse, when using a weapon such as his bow. While the first few weeks were overwhelming and exhausting, Samuel quickly picked up on this training and soon was up almost as early as Lowman, who was always ready to begin his next lesson.

He'd grown an additional three inches since he first arrived.

"They are here," Gabram said as Samuel turned to face him. He knew, seeing Gabram in his silk blue Patron's robe, that this day was going to be different. "Could it be?" he thought.

"Get your things together," Gabram instructed. "We have a long ride ahead of us today."

So Samuel returned to his room and changed into clothes suitable for riding.

"One more thing," Gabram said when Samuel came back to the main room. "I was asked to give this to you." He stretched out his hand, which held a small wooden case.

As Samuel extended his hand to receive it, his eyes caught the ring on Gabram's finger. The ring seemed to pulsate with flashes of lightning. He'd never seen Gabram wearing the ring before around the house. As soon as the case rested on his palm, it made a clicking sound, which caused Samuel to flinch, almost dropping it.

"What is it?" he asked, his curiosity piqued.

"That is for you to share," Gabram replied.

Samuel opened the unlocked box, revealing a silver necklace with a black centerpiece that rested perfectly inside the case. The rectangular-shaped piece was intricately designed, with a single arrow encircling it like a serpent.

Samuel thought there was something familiar about it, like a lost memory he should remember.

"Iseac wanted you to have it," Gabram said. "Go ahead, put it on."

So Samuel did, placing it around his neck with the centerpiece resting on his chest.

"We'd better get going, then," Gabram said, walking past Samuel, who followed.

They rode from dawn until the sun was past its zenith

when Mount Va'lenna came into view between the trees. As they trotted up the spiraling mountainside, Samuel placed his hand over his forehead to shield his eyes from the sun.

As they got higher, Samuel could see four large pillars that supported a larger piece overhead. Each pillar had a symbol on it, but he couldn't make out what they were because of the angle of the glaring sun. They soon arrived at the magnificent structure on top of the mountain. A side gate led into a courtyard, with the main entrance to the building on their left.

Everyone, from the moment they rode in, greeted Gabram as he passed by, and he courteously nodded his head in response.

They made their way from the stable to a massive double door that dwarfed those close to it. When the door closed behind them, it seemed to shut them off from the world. Gabram took off his shoes, as did Samuel, and they were handed damp towels by two young men standing at the entrance to an open room off the main hallway. The young men stood there, waiting to take away their towels when they were finished.

Once done, they made their way along the hallway. Samuel started feeling nervous, not sure if he was ready for what was going to happen next. As if sensing Samuel's tension from the way he was looking around, like a bird ready to take flight,

Gabram began to speak.

"We are heading to the Council room, which is going to be on our right."

"The place is amazing," Samuel thought as he continued to admire the tranquil beauty of the building. It had a tan marble floor that was an extension to the one on the wall that rose to his shoulder, covering every passageway. The rest of the wall from his shoulder up was midnight blue, like the sky without any clouds. Fire crystals like starlight were set several feet apart along the way.

"Remember, the Patrons are here for you," Gabram said. He led Samuel to a double door that was intricately designed.

"Wait here until you are summoned. Don't worry, you will be fine," Gabram said before going in.

* * * * *

In the circle of Patrons, Thorlak, the chief Patron asked, "Is he ready?"

"Yes, he is ready," Gabram replied.

"Everyone needs at least two years to prepare," Buldric said. "We all know this could kill him."

"Yes, it could," Gabram said. "But there is a reason he was chosen by the Anamerian. I do not know why, but I feel he can do it."

Some of the Patrons were concerned and, to a degree,

shared Buldric's view, even though they said nothing. No one had ever been presented in such a short period of time before, but they all accepted Gabram's judgment, nodding their heads to show their willingness to proceed.

"Very well," Thorlak said. "Since there are no objections, let us proceed." A voice whispered in Samuel's ear as he stood outside the chamber waiting. It wasn't a familiar voice, but he knew that was his cue. He took in a deep breath just before he pushed the doors open and walked inside.

The door closed behind him as he made his way to the center of the circular dome-like room. The room was so quiet that he heard the sound of his own heartbeat. He saw the Patrons sitting on straight-backed marble chairs that rose over their heads. Each chair was built from the ground up with white marble that made each Patron appear dreamlike as he sat waiting.

He felt their eyes on him as he stopped in the middle of the circle facing the chief Patron, as he was instructed by Gabram.

The room, like the rest of the building, was cool and crisp. When the chief Patron spoke, his voice filled the Great Hall. "The Anamerian has found the first, and Gabram has set his path," he said ritualistically.

"'We have come united to unseal, that heart and mind out

of the darkness might see, the truth once known to all revealed.

"And I so freely offer," the chief Patron concluded.

"And I so freely offer," Gabram said, as did each person in the room.

Cyriac was the last Patron to join in agreement, and when he was done, Samuel responded, "I accept the gift so freely given." And then there was silence.

The light in the room slowly became dim, and Samuel suddenly felt alone. A surge of energy like a drop of rain before a storm started building around him. His body drew on the source of the energy; he had no control of it as it ran through every part of his being. The energy settled in his head with an intensity that could only be compared to a plum smashed against a rock.

Samuel felt his mind being seared like silk in a furnace, unlocking unknown chambers in his mind. He screamed and dropped down to his knees while grabbing onto his head and trembling uncontrollably. His heart pounded as if it were going to rip out of his chest. His eyes were shut, squeezed from pain, but underneath the pain, a sweeter sensation followed of equal intensity.

Memories once part of him flooded his mind like a tidal wave as a new fabric began to weave itself inside his mind, with old ones burning away.

Samuel continued to tremble as the physical manifestations of the changes going on inside his mind started to appear externally. Each hair on his head, beginning at the roots, slowly began to change into silver as if he was being cleansed from inside. When he opened his eyes again, they glowed like the moon, as they too had changed.

The arrow around the centerpiece on his necklace unlaced itself to reveal a sky-blue crystal, and the single arrow split into two straight ones resting on opposite sides of a now pure silver frame.

Samuel slowly rose from the floor, but it was a different person looking around the room. He had a slight smile on his face as if waking from a dream. He had a silvery aura around him like the moon in the shape of his adult self. When he spoke, it was the sound of a thousand men held within the bounds of a young man's voice, but it carried the strength of one not bound by mortality. His lips did not move as he addressed the Patrons, staring into their eyes.

The Samuel that now stood in front of them could see in their faces the energy he'd had to pull from them for his awakening, but the Patrons all held themselves up, their faces hiding the strain he could feel from them.

"I can sense an inbalance, and it is all around us," the thing inside Samuel said. "The Anamerian is alive, even though my sense of him is fading due to his wavering link; it makes it difficult to tell where he's being held. What does the Council know about the shift?"

"Bollan, Nor, Tylan, and Kathleen, protected by the marble seal, have vanished, and one of them has taken the Anamerian," the chief Patron said.

"I will find him and my brothers," referring to the two others like him, and he began walking to the door.

"Great Lord of the Moon," the chief Patron spoke with the reverence of a servant, stopping Samuel in his tracks. He turned to look at Thorlak with his eyes shining bright.

"My Lord, if I may so freely speak, I do not think the people are ready. You might want to keep it on the crystal," Thorlak said. "And your men will be waiting to follow when you are ready."

Samuel had forgotten he was still glowing and would have drawn the attention of everyone in the building.

"*Tora fanarum*," he said and the glow around him faded, leaving only his dim silver eyes. He walked out the room with the Patrons staring at a true Ackalan, endowed with the power contained within the scrolls of creation.

At that point, they remembered the third record from the prophecies of Ryham: 'They shall again return on that day when men shall lose all hope, scarred from the whips of bondage and death. On their backs will they carry the wings of freedom for all men.' They all knew that day was truly upon them.

Chapter 24

The Spark of Hope

Two men dressed in ashen gray stood watching as Iseac tried to stop himself from falling over after being shoved into a room he thought was empty. He'd been held against a wall next to an open door a few minutes before while the lock around his neck was removed. The guard did not follow as they shoved him in through the door.

As Iseac tried to stop himself from falling, an invisible band clasped his hands and feet, holding him in place. He looked up from the slick, salty-colored looking floor to see the two men with their faces hiding in the cowl of their cloaks. The room would have been bright were it not for the patches of gray on the walls. Apparently they had being watching him the whole time.

Iseac watched as one of the figures approached with his hand still locked in place, unable to move. He recognized the red ring on the figure's finger and knew right away who it was. He was the man who was going to end Elena's life in front of him. As the man moved his hands up, Iseac's own arm went up in unison until his shoes barely touched the floor.

Iseac stared into the cowl of the former Patron's hood as he walked toward him, not intimidated as he held on tightly to the anger burning inside him.

The man moved close to Iseac and then slowly walked around, stopping behind him. With his lips next to Iseac's ear, he said in a cold whisper, "I hope you are as strong as your predecessors."

As those words left his lips, a sudden chill ran down Iseac's spine and his eyes suddenly bulged from the Patron's touch. A sharp pain burrowed into his skull and he began to convulse. With each violent shake, a web of red veins began to form along the edges of his eyes just before they rolled in the back of his head. His head suddenly dropped down, the pain knocking him unconscious.

Satisfied with his result, the former Patron released his grip around Iseac's neck. He took in a deep breath, shifting his shoulder in and out as he exhaled, appearing to have drawn strength from Iseac. A drop of blood slid down Iseac's nose as the Patron released his hold, letting Iseac's limp body drop to the ground.

"As long as he's alive, we should be able to find them," the former Patron said to his companion, who walked over to check on Iseac. "Get the men together," the former Patron instructed.

His companion nodded his head in response and began

making his way to the door when his name was called.

"Rogan." The man stopped. "I will be joining you and the men this time, and send one of the guards to get him," the former Patron said.

"It shall be done," Rogan replied.

****

When Iseac regained consciousness, he was lying on his back. He squeezed his eyes and blinked several times to clear his vision. His head throbbed and he felt as if he'd been trodden underfoot by a herd of cattle. Disoriented and not thinking straight, Iseac tried to sit up. Every part of his body fought against it, and he lost consciousness and dropped to the floor.

When he opened his eyes the next day, he was still weak, but not as before, and his mind was somewhat clear. As he sat up, his body reminded him that all was not well. The pain in his head was now a dull ache. He gingerly placed his hand at the back of his neck to assess the damage he'd received at the hands of the former Patron. He rubbed his hand gently against his skin; it felt stiff and bruised, but the skin wasn't broken. He looked at his fingers–there was no blood.

Knowing this did not make any difference in the way he felt. He remembered the Patron's touch at the back of his neck and the intense pain, as if someone was drilling a hole in his skull. While he was glad to be alive, something was amiss. He was being held in his original cell. The place was quiet and empty of his neighboring cellmates, which meant they were either working or being fed. While Iseac was thinking about what they may have done to him, he remembered: Elena!

That thought wiped out every other concern. He needed to find her; he had to make sure she was okay.

Getting down on one knee, he placed his hand on the floor. He recited a few words and gained sight beyond his cell. Just as it began, it was drawn somewhere else and winked out. He tried again, and the same thing happened. He began to panic. For the first time, Iseac truly felt afraid. Taking a deep breath, he slowly began to clear his mind, concentrating on his core.

Everything around him faded away like a fog dispelled by the sun. The damp cave wall, the choking smell of smoke and dirt, and everything around him seemed distant.

He was at the heart of his core, feeling every connection in his mind. At first everything appeared normal, but as he dug deeper, he began to see what had been done to him. New webs were rooted into the edges of his mind—not his own, but a taint that was now part of him. He did not understand how it was possible, but now he knew the reason why he felt different and unable to concentrate.

Still puzzled by his discovery, Iseac felt a prickling in his mind and a different fear came over him. A surge of silver light rushed toward his core, enveloping his thoughts before he could retreat. The energy was like a lightning bolt, and inside it stood a young man. Iseac squinted, shielding his vision to peer at the figure in his core.

He recognized the face as it turned to look at him. It was Samuel. The figure did not see him, but he could sense Samuel felt his presence, like the last time they met in Chartum-Valley.

Iseac opened his eyes, shocked and amazed that such powers were able to penetrate his core, allowing him a glimpse of an event that was happening. "Samuel!" he muttered. It couldn't be...but it was, and hope once again lit up inside him.

Chapter 25

Keeper of the Gate

At Mount Va'lenna, it was dark outside and the cool evening breeze stilled the air as a young man stepped out of Rod Stone temple.

"Samuel!" a familiar voice called. He turned to see Mosley walking toward him, and he smiled as he approached.

"It is good to see you well and alive," Mosley said.

"It is good to see you, too," Samuel replied, bowing his head.

"Where is Iseac?" Samuel asked.

"He was taken captive before we could reach him." Mosley's tone reflected his disappointment. "After you left..." he began, and went on to narrate all that had transpired after Samuel rode off into the woods. He also told him about the Agoras that were captured as they tried to flee the scene. The Agoras were being held for questioning.

"What about you?" Mosley asked. "We heard that you made it safely to Gabram."

"Yes." Samuel told him about his encounter with the Golans, how he had narrowly escaped with his life, and how lucky he was to have found a ship heading directly from

Lufgard to Bremah, where Gabram was waiting for him.

"The gods must be with you," Mosley said, since ships rarely go directly from Lufgard to Bremah. "I'm glad the Patron got the message before you arrived...come with me. There is someone I would like you to meet." He placed a hand on Samuel's shoulder and led him to the Ackalans' quarters, which was a building to the left of the temple on the opposite side of the stable.

Inside the Ackalans' quarters was a straight hallway that went through three rooms. The first room had rows of benches and tables; it was the dining area. The Ackalans who were eating at the tables gave them a quick glance before turning their attention back to their food. As they made their way past the second room, Samuel could see rows of mats and pillows. Some of the beds were being used by Ackalans who had traveled there as escorts to the Patrons who came for his unlocking. No one appeared to be paying them any attention, but if you looked closer, you would see that each man's weapon was as good as drawn, with how close it rested by their beds.

The last room had two doors on opposite ends of the wall; in the middle of this room was an oval-shaped altar that was wide enough to accommodate four people.

Two men were looking over something on top of it. As

soon as Samuel and Mosely approached the third entrance, the men turned to face them.

"Ashra," Mosley said. "I would like you to meet Samuel from Chartum-Valley."

The man standing in front of him was tall with broad shoulders. His eyes were dark brown with the silver rings that were common with all Ackalans. Along his chiseled face hung two single braids and his muscular form was well defined underneath his clothes.

"It is nice to meet you, Samuel of Chartum-Valley. *Kru haya no-nah.* "I'm Tremay. This is Hildra, my second in command."

Hildra, an older man with more gray than black in his hair, nodded in the same manner as Tremay.

"We first received word over a year ago of a occurrence similar to what happened to your people in Chartum-Valley," Tremay said. "The people in a small village suddenly disappeared without a trace.

"Rumor back then was that the villagers were cursed, since no one had a rational explanation. Since then, there has been a steady rise of these unexplained disappearances and without any witnesses—at least, until you.

"The disappearances, from what we've gathered so far, have been random, from small villages to large ones with population of over two thousand. We do see a pattern. They are moving closer to bigger towns like yours."

"While their actions may appear random," Samuel said, "I believe they are searching for the same people as the Anamerian, which was why they were in Chartum-Valley and why they captured Iseac. The Anamerian is important in all of this, and that is why I leave tonight to begin my search for him."

If they were impressed by Samuel's confidence, none of them showed it. Mosley looked at him, not sure if he was the same scared, unsure young man he met just over a year ago. Now he spoke with the confidence of a warrior.

"We were asked to go with you when you are ready, and we have been waiting," Tremay said. "The Patrons asked that we share this information with you." Tremay turned to the table, where there was an open map of the four Kingdoms. He pointed to an area south of Po'trema on the map.

"From the information Adal was able to gather from the Agoras, we believe the Anamerian might be held here," he said, his finger close to Amito-Mountain. The land of the sun, Samuel thought.

Samuel nodded his head several times as Tremay spoke about the surrounding area. The wasteland was a perfect site, with weather so harsh and unforgiving no one who escaped could survive. However, what caught Samuel's attention, and reaffirmed the Patron's suggestion, was what Tremay said about the mountain pass: rumors of monstrous creatures possessing, killing, or snatching people at night.

If this was really happening, Samuel thought, then the scale of the world has truly been tipped and this kind of event is a result of an imbalance in all things.

"Ashra," Samuel asked, "how long will it take your men to be ready?"

"Ten minutes," Tremay said.

"Good...we leave tonight, and I need to prepare. Peace and prosperity, Ashra." Samuel said in the old tongue as he bowed his head.

Impressed by his use of the old tongue, which very few knew, Tremay responded in the same manner before they left to make preparations.

Within ten minutes, as Tremay said, they were ready and waiting. When Samuel stepped out of the temple doors again, he was dressed in a dark-blue shirt with silver embroidery along the cuff and chest. His trousers and boots were black and his cloak was dark brown. He held a silver longbow and arrows that seemed to gleam in the dark.

The Patrons were standing by the door as he walked over to Tremay with his eyes glowing, a mirror of the moonlight.

"Ashra, have your men dismount and follow me," Samuel instructed. He waited for his instruction to be passed along before he began making his way back to the temple doors, which were pulled open as he approached.

If the Ackalans were curious, none of them showed it. Adal and Thorlak stood waiting as they approached the door to the room holding one of the scrolls of creation. When they were all close enough to hear him, Samuel spoke up.

"Everyone stay around the wall when we go inside and form a circle around me. Place your hand on the shoulder of the person to your right. It will make what we are about to do easier on everyone." With that, Samuel turned to look at the Patron, nodding his signal for them to open the door. It was like a door to another world in a room that was as bright as the evening sky with all the stars.

Samuel walked toward the middle as everyone else filed in. His form began to change as the last person walked in and the door closed behind them. In the darkened room, they could all see the soft silvery aura that was forming around him.

As Samuel took an arrow from its quiver, it changed into pure silver. He aimed and released the arrow into the glowing ball at the heart of the pool. In a flash, it split into four before driving into the ball at perfect angles. The arrows started spinning. With each rotation, the pool got brighter and brighter. Everyone began to stare at the water.

It became so bright that they all had to shield their eyes, but Samuel watched as the scroll rose from inside the pool into the air. It wasn't long before it was hovering above them.

The light that filled the room began to gather into a single pillar of light that slowly took form, changing into an illuminated figure in the center of the pool. Her garment, like her, was almost translucent white, and she beamed like the sun. She took in everyone in the room at a glance, but her eyes came to rest on Samuel.

"I am the keeper of the gate," she announced in a soft whisper, her words sinking deep into every part of their being. "It has been over a thousand years. Is your path set?"

"Yes, our path is clear and we are ready to enter," Samuel replied, following an ancient protocol.

"Then let not body and mind bind the way," she said, moving toward Samuel. She touched him at the center of his chest with one of her fingers, and then she was gone.

The room became dimmer again, but the pool was still lit, and the aura around Samuel became brighter than before. Samuel's eyes became open from the keeper's touch. He could see patches of green close to a mountainside, as if looking through a window, and he recognized the place as Amito-Mountain.

He closed his eyes and felt everything around the room shift. When he opened his eyes again, they were all standing outside.

Samuel looked out onto the rugged plain as a gentle breeze blew past his face. He knew exactly where they were; they had made it.

Chapter 26

Dead End

"We are here," Samuel announced to the Ackalans, who stood in a circle still holding onto their companion's shoulder. While they may not have understood it before, they now saw the wisdom in Samuel's request that they hold onto one another's shoulder as they flashed out of and back into reality. One of the men in the circle threw up from nausea. As everyone in their own subtle way were reassuring themselves of the reality of their new position, Tremay, who seemed unperturbed by their experience, broke away from their circle and walked over to Samuel.

It was still dark out, but the moon provided enough light for them to see the sparsely forested area around them. The air was warm and dry for the time of day, a reminder that they were in the desert.

"Something is wrong," Samuel thought, and it wasn't that he could sense Iseac close and far at the same time, as if there were two of him.

"We need to be vigilant; there are living and non-living moving around this place," Samuel announced before they began moving.

They walked quietly to the right of Amito–Mountain when they saw a fog appear in the distance. Even at a distance, something about it did not look right. They watched it drift toward them till they were enveloped by it. The fog held the rancid smell of things that were decaying as they moved cautiously along. The mist wasn't extremely dense, but it impeded their view slightly. Just a few feet in, they heard it: the faint sound of something approaching. While they could see nothing, the sound was getting louder as it drew closer.

"Everyone, stay here," Samuel said in a voice that was almost as godly as the gatekeeper. In the mist they could see his glowing figure as he darted away with inhuman speed, disappearing into the mist.

Samuel stopped about a hundred yards away from the Ackalans. He took out an arrow, nocked, and pulled, watching as figures appeared in the fog. As their impression became clearer, Samuel could see that they were Qui-Mas, creatures denied the peace of death. The Qui-Mas were charging in their direction, weapons drawn, pulled by the scent of blood.

Fifty yards from his position, Samuel released a string of arrows in rapid succession. As each silver arrow took flight, it split into a dozen, with each hitting its intended target. The force from each arrow was like a lightning bolt, striking two or three at a time. The creatures dropped to the ground, pilling the earth as they rolled to a stop with dust rising around them. Those that were struck immediately started decaying until they crumbled into dust.

One of the creatures slipped past Samuel on his left flank while the others slowly halted, screaming from their positions as they waved their weapons in the air. They could all see the glowing figure in the distance with bow and arrow drawn and unmoved by their screaming. With so many dead around them, they decided after several minutes to retreat. Just as they had appeared with the mist, they faded away.

Just as the mist was beginning to disperse, Tremay saw a creature twice his size appear with its blade raised, ready to strike him. Tremay's sword was already drawn when a flash of silver zipped overhead. The creature squalled as it dropped to the ground and immediately started decaying.

"They are called Qui-Mas, or cursed souls," Samuel said. "They are people stuck between our world and the next. They possess and reshape the bodies of wild animals, and they will be back." Those words drew everyone's attention back to Samuel.

"Normal steel is useless against them. Anything they touch before withering to this state, they can possess, till the thing or person is killed.

"We better get going," Samuel said in his normal tone with

the brightness in his eyes slowly diminishing. He began walking back the way he had come, with Tremay following beside him.

"I may have found our entrance," Samuel said. "Those mounds are underground vents; they were crafted to look like natural rock formations, but if you look closely, you will see that they are too evenly spaced to be sporadic. Whoever did this did not want to be noticed, even in the desert. Hopefully we will leave as unnoticed as we came."

Samuel pointed to one of the mounds among the vast numbers spread across the land.

"That one," he said, and three of the Ackalans placed their hands underneath the exposed part of the disk-shaped mound, tipping it on its side to reveal a hole the size of a cart wheel.

Samuel dropped one of his arrows into the hole, counting until it hit the ground. Since it wasn't deep, he jumped in and called for the others to join him, which they did in succession, calling for the next person once they were out of the way.

The first thing they noticed inside was the rancid smell that clung in the air. The area around them was covered with broken tools and dirt mingled with human remains that were pushed against the corners of the cave.

"He is here," Samuel said. From what he could see, they were enclosed, except for a small section that appeared to be boarded.

He walked over to the boards, not completely sure what to do, but he placed his hand on the wood and concentrated. Nothing happened at first; then he saw a subtle ripple as the boards suddenly expanded and collapsed into shreds.

Samuel grabbed a handful of the pieces of wood. They turned silvery and stretched out into perfect arrows that he placed in his quiver.

Behind the boards was a passageway, as Samuel had hoped, and he walked into the dark tunnel with the Ackalans following. For several minutes, they walked in pitch blackness.

"Thousands of people are being held here, and we are not to be seen or noticed," Tremay said, making it clear that their purpose was only to get the Anamerian.

Staying within the shadows, they made their way through areas that were partly lit, unnoticed until they came to an open exit. Samuel raised his hand, stopping everyone behind him. He peeked into a vast canyon and spotted three armed figures with wolfish eyes on the opposite side of a suspended bridge. A dozen armed Agoras were crossing the bridge and heading their way.

Samuel had been calm up to this point, but that disappeared when he saw the Agoras that were heading their way. Distinct memories of Elye dying, with an arrow in his chest, flooded his mind. The loss of his father and brothers to these monsters pushed him over the edge, and with an uncontrollable rage, he stepped out into the open. He reached for an arrow, but there were now only shreds of wood. One of them pricked his finger, but he felt nothing except anger. The glow that was once around his eyes was gone.

The Agoras seemed surprised, but before they could react, Tremay and the Ackalans leaped into the open from the corners where they were hiding, as if from thin air. Within minutes, the Agoras were all brought down.

Samuel stood there, angry for not being able to take revenge for his family. His emotions drove away any concern about their mission or the advantage of stealth they had just lost. His anger burned like hot steel against the world. He did not care about his ability failing. They had been spotted by the three armed figures who were charging across the bridge to meet them. Six of the Ackalans rushed to meet the Norians, their weapons still covered with the blood of the Agoras.

"Are you all right?" Mosley asked Samuel, who was still enraged.

"I'm not sure."

"We need to go," he said, tapping Samuel on the shoulder. His touch pushed Samuel into motion, and he ran after Mosley toward the bridge.

All this time Samuel thought he had control, but seeing the Agoras brought the memory of his loss back like a wound reopen. Across the bridge, Samuel's rage was still subsiding as he walked past two Ackalans that were pulling away one of the dead Norians. The second Norian was being moved to a dark corner of the cave, away from the entrance that they were once guarding.

As Samuel walked into the tunnel, he remembered initially spotting three. Where was the third? They hadn't traveled far when he spotted the last Norian sprawled on the ground. He drew his eyes away from the creature.

Tremay called to him as he was unlocking a cell."Over here."

Samuel rushed down the slight slope to a cage built into the wall. Inside the cage was a man covered in dirt, but he recognized the face immediately. Iseac.

His hair was tangled in dirt and his cheeks hollow, with his eyes sunken. His clothes were in tatters and he looked at them in shock.

He walked inside. "I did it."

"Samuel," Iseac said, his voice rusty, "I wasn't sure if the connection I was feeling was true until I saw you standing there. I guess I'm not as crazy as I thought. Help me up. There is someone I need to find. She is being held here because of me."

"We will come back for everyone else later," Tremay said, "but first we must get you to safety."

"No!" Iseac replied with as much strength he could muster, trying to pull away. "I would rather die than leave her here," he thought.

"I know where she is," Iseac said instead, as he leaned against Samuel. "Follow me."

In the dark from behind iron bars, eyes stared at them. It showed the faces of people who had lost all hope, too frightened to act on their own. No one reached out or cried for help; they just stared in silence.

They made their way through an open area. In the center, steps rose into what looked like an altar at the top, all made of marble. The Ackalans scanned the area as they made their way around it.

"Two guard her door," Iseac said before they turned into the hallway.

"Wait here," Tremay said, signaling for three of his men to come with him. It wasn't long before they heard the thudding sound as the monstrous charge they could hear was cut off.

"Now," Tremay said and they made their way to a thick wooden door. One of the Ackalans unlocked it with the key he had taken from one of the creatures and pushed the door open.

Iseac let go of Samuel and walked into the room.

"It's me, Iseac," he announced as he leaned down to help Elena, who looked at him, surprised. She took his hand for support and they walked out of the room. She was younger than him, from what Samuel could tell, and like Iseac, she too was covered in dirt.

"Do you know a way out of here?" Tremay asked.

"No," Iseac replied.

"Then we head back," Tremay said, turning when Elena spoke up.

"I know a way, and it's not far from here," she said.

"Show me," Tremay said in that commanding voice that demanded absolute obedience, and they made their way back, taking a different exit at the grand room with the marbled tile.

As they hurried through the tunnel, Samuel couldn't help but wonder if his brother and mother were here, too, and alive.

The part of the tunnel they were now taking was different. The farther in they went, the more spread apart the fire posts became until they were in complete darkness.

At the end of the tunnel was a heavy wooden door inlaid with iron. They only needed to use the pulley to roll the chain up in order to open the gate. Two of the men ran over to begin opening the gate, and that was when they discovered the missing piece. A single rod that locked the chain, which held the pulley in place, was missing. Without it, they were at a dead end and needed to find another way.

Chapter 27

Hope Rekindled

It was obvious that they could not use this exit unless they had the rod, so they began making their way back. As they passed the first sets of cells, which had five sections, Samuel thought he heard the faint voice of someone calling his name.

"Must be my imagination," he said to himself. Then he heard it again. It was weak, but he did hear it. He knew only someone from his town would recognize or know him by name.

He turned and began frantically making his way back in the general direction they had come as Mosley and another Ackalan ran up after him. Samuel hoped that whoever it was knew something about his family and where they might be. He searched through the faces in the first cell he came to.

No one looked familiar, so he hurried to the next one, but again he did not recognize any of the faces. Was his mind playing tricks on him? He was beginning to wonder as he moved to the third. No one there looked familiar, either; resting both hands on the iron bars, discouraged, Samuel looked down and saw a young man with dark hair.

"Who called my name?" he asked, not caring that his

words were projecting, his tone edged with frustration.

No one answered. As he turned to leave, someone spoke up.

"Him," the person said, pointing to a figure on the ground. The person on the ground raised his head and the expression on Samuel's face changed.

"Over here," Samuel cried, dropping to his knees as everyone else wondered what he was doing.

Mosley was the first one to reach Samuel.

"Open the gate," Samuel instructed. "It is my brother."

The gate was barely open when Samuel rushed to Faray, ecstatic. Faray was still getting to his feet when Samuel swung his arms around him, lifting him off the ground. Nothing at that moment mattered, even as everyone inside and outside the cell stood watching them.

"I thought I had lost you."

"I thought I had lost you, too," Faray replied.

"We have to leave now," Mosley said, interrupting both of them. Samuel released his hands around his brother.

"Where is Mother?" he asked, overlooking Faray's state, who had visible scars all over his gaunt body with his tattered clothes hanging loosely on him.

"She did not make it," he said regretfully. "And there was nothing I could do."

Not wanting to dwell on what he could not change, Samuel asked. "Can you walk?"

"Yes, with some help."

"Good!" Samuel said, knowing they weren't safe yet. "Then we need to go."

He placed one of Faray's arms over his shoulder and was starting to head out when Faray spoke up.

"Stop!" he said and Samuel did.

"We have to help them." Samuel had forgotten about the other prisoners, whom he now recognized as being from Chartum-Valley. The prisoners' eyes begged to be free.

"You can all come with us if you can keep up," he announced in a voice loud enough for everyone in the cell to hear.

"They know we are here and are coming!" Iseac said, cutting in right after Samuel, his tone emphasizing the urgency for them to get going. "We cannot head that way," he said, pointing in the direction they were heading.

"Then we will go back," Samuel said in response.

"You know we don't have the missing piece," Iseac said.

"I know, and I think I can get that door open."

It was as if finding his brother had given him a new hope. Without further questions, they hurriedly made their way back. As they did, Samuel started clearing his mind.

"I need everyone to stop and wait here," Samuel instructed a few yards from the gate. He let go of Faray, who had been leaning on him for support, and walked into the dark alone. Using Gabram's lessons, he slowly began the process of connecting to his true self.

The Ackalans watched and listened for signs of their coming assailants. It wasn't long before they heard it–the sound of heavy boots heading their way with increasing speed; they were closing in on them fast.

The Ackalans stood, ready for whatever was coming, while everyone else stood behind them. Suddenly they saw a soft glow in the area that was once pitch black.

"Over there," a voice from with the small group said, pointing in Samuel's direction. Soon they all turned, except the Ackalans, who were focused on those that were coming. Everyone else stared in amazement at the glow.

His aura was in the shape of a grown man. His eyes were bright and his hair glowed like pure silver. He took an arrow from his quiver and placed it on his bow, which he pointed just over the group's head and released. The arrow disappeared in a flash, splitting midflight like lightning bolts. A loud thudding sound, followed a second later by the sound of things dropping to the ground, reverberating off the tunnel wall. Samuel took the rest of the arrows except two from his quiver. In a twisting motion, he molded the arrows into the shape of the missing rod.

Locking them in place, he began to spin the wheel. With each rotation, the gate grindingly began to rise as streams of light and a gust of cool air flowed into the tunnel.

"Everyone out," Samuel commanded in a voice that filled the cave. It wasn't a loud voice, but they all felt it. The group started running, all shielding their eyes as they emerged out of the cave.

Their assailants had stopped running, but they were still making their way toward them.

Faray, like everyone around him, could not hide the shock in his face. It wasn't just the mystery of his brother's transformation. How far had he shot, he wondered, knowing that Norians were fast creatures and should have been upon them by now. He had seen them dash from one side of the tunnel to the other within minutes. He had a lot of questions, but for now they were free and his younger brother was still alive, and that was enough.

When Iseac looked at Samuel, he could only think of the silver statues he remembered holding as a boy in the cave; "the statue with the arrow," he said to himself, and he knew now, more than ever, that he needed to find the other two. If the others could do the same things as Samuel, he couldn't imagine what would happen if they were captured and used by Sullivan.

Once they were all out, including Samuel, he waved his hand. The gate rolled down, slamming shut with a force that caused a puff of dust to rise at the base.

"Hopefully no one will be able to use that exit for a while," Samuel hoped. He turned and began making his way to the others, with his eyes and form slowly changing back to normal.

Elena could not believe Iseac came for her. Somehow, he had found a way. And even though they had no provisions, she was confident they would survive. For now she was happy to be with Iseac, and she squeezed his hand.

It was still morning, and the sun was already warming the cool desert. They had made it out without any casualties. As they looked around, the knowledge of where they were sank in. Their exit had put them at the edge of the desert, with no shade in sight, and the sun was rising.

Their captors had purposefully assigned some of the prisoners to work in this area so they could see that even if they somehow managed to escape, there would be nowhere to go, and they would die in the desert. They made sure enough people worked outside to see what their fate would be, hoping the word would spread. So it was no surprise to them that they ended up on this side of the tunnel, since it was the only way out they were aware of.

"We need to find shade before the sun gets high enough in the sky," Tremay said, as if reading Samuel's thoughts.

"Iseac, do you know of a location near our current position where we can find some shade?" Samuel asked.

Anamerians were living maps, and Samuel hoped Iseac knew of a place where they could find refuge from the sun.

"Yes," Iseac said. "Follow me," and they began making their way in the opposite direction, away from the desert.

As they made their way across the barren landscape, Iseac hoped they were all ready for what was coming. The thing that had been perching in his mind seemed to have come alive since their escape. While he could not explain what was happening to him, he could feel something coming, and he realized that could only mean one thing.

"I need to speak with Samuel and Tremay alone for a minute," he said to Elena, who was standing by his side, her fingers twined in his. "Please get Samuel for me."

She released her fingers from his and made her way over to Samuel.

"Iseac would like to speak with you," she informed Samuel, who was walking with Faray.

"Of course, I will be back in a minute," he said to Faray.

Since their escape, Tremay had made sure he or Hildra,

discreetly stayed close to Iseac. He wasn't going to lose him again.

When Samuel arrived, Iseac told them about the former Patron who was behind his capture. He did not bother to describe the former Patron; it wasn't relevant at the time. The point was, they now knew what was coming and needed to prepare.

"He did something to me," Iseac continued, "that somehow allows him to see and know the same things I know."

It now made sense to Samuel why it felt as if Iseac were at two different places at the same time.

"He is coming and we need to be prepared," Iseac said.

"I will take care of them."

"No! He already knows about your ability through me, and I believe that is why they are coming."

"For me," Samuel said.

"Yes...but I have a plan." They listened as Iseac explained. "And we need to find somewhere safe for these people," Iseac continued, thinking of Elena. "The people in the tunnel get their water from a natural spring not far from our position, but we will need to get them there as fast as we can."

"I will get the men ready, and this is yours," Tremay said, handing Iseac his quarterstaff before making his way to Hildra.

"Samuel, the spring is buried deep in the ground. Do you

think you can access it?"

"I'll try."

"Good, then we better get going," Iseac said, sounding like his old self with his controlled demeanor.

It soon became clear to Iseac that at the pace the former Patron and his men were approaching, they wouldn't make it to the spring. Most of the slaves were weak and the sun was beginning to drain their remaining strength. They would have to carry out their plans before reaching their destination.

Chapter 28

Course of Action

Grains of desert sand subtly shifted under their feet before they heard it: the faint sound of a large mass heading their way. They did not have to guess who or what would be about at this time of day, several hours after their escape. They could only hope it wasn't what they were thinking, even though in their hearts they suspected otherwise.

The air was getting warmer as the sun edged out of the horizon, and they looked to their rescuers for what to do next. They stopped moving and murmured amongst themselves.

There were thirty-two people in their band, including Iseac, Elena, Samuel, Faray, the sixteen Ackalans, and a dozen freed prisoners. Within the group of prisoners were three women, a young boy about ten years of age, an older man around sixty-five, and the rest were in their twenties to later thirties.

Tremay broke away from the pack of Ackalans and made his way to the freed prisoners.

"How many of you can handle a weapon?" he asked.

Seven raised their hands, including the oldest man in their group, Faray, and a young girl who said she was good with the bow.

"Step forward," Tremay commanded, gesturing to the volunteers. As they did, they were joined by a young boy who ran up a second later.

"Hildra, take them away," Tremay instructed. "And young man," he said to the boy, "you stay with me." Hildra herded the others toward the Ackalans.

"Everyone, listen," Tremay said, drawing the attention of those who remained. "We are going to be splitting into two groups. You will remain here while the rest of us find out what lies ahead. Someone will bring word if it is safe to continue, so do not worry."

Tremay turned to look at the boy by his side. His face softened.

"What is your name?"

"Jude," the boy replied.

"This weapon, Jude," Tremay said, pulling out a shortsword, "was made by a master craftsman and has been in my family for generations. Only three of its kind were made in the Kingdom. It will protect you like it has me, and those staying here that you will be guarding when we're gone." He handed Jude the shortsword."Will you protect these people?"

Jude nodded his head, looking at the weapon that seemed to absorb the light. He looked at Tremay, unsure what to say.

"Go on," Tremay said, urging him along, and Jude ran

back to the others.

The Ackalans carried more than their fair share of weapons. When the seven prisoners returned a few minutes later, they were armed. Four of them would remain behind with the group, including the girl, who was now armed with a silver bow and arrows that could only have been made by Samuel.

"As long as I'm alive, this weapon will not fail you until I remove the bond that binds it to me," he had told her. The other three, including Faray, would come with them to head off whatever was coming.

"You will be safe here till I return," Iseac told Elena as they prepared to leave. She hugged him, planting a kiss on his cheek.

"Be careful," she said, and soon they were off.

By the time their enemies came into view, they had just moved far enough for the others to be out of sight. Ahead of them, a growing number of armed creatures appeared over the horizon. Their numbers increased as they drew closer, spreading across a large area. From Iseac's estimation, there were roughly two thousand of these creatures known as Norians. There was no cover on the open plain, just an ocean of sand.

"Today is going to be the day that I'll have to put all my

training into action, but first I need to level the playing field so we'll have a fighting chance," Iseac thought as a gust of warm desert breeze blew around them. He would use the natural resources available to them.

Iseac could make out the armed Norians, who looked like boulders with their gray skin and massive weapons. Behind them were Golans on horseback, with their faces painted for battle. At the head of the groups was the former Patron, with Rogan by his side, both of them on horseback. Like Thorlak, the former Patron spoke to Iseac telepathically. Even in his head the voice sent a chill down Iseac's spine.

"I know he is here," the former Patron said sinuously. "I can feel him, just like you. If you send him to me, I might let you live and maybe spare your family, too."

"I think you must be confused," Iseac replied, as if he wasn't just threatened. "You and your master will pay for the innocent lives you've destroyed, and it will begin with you."

"Ah ha ha..." the former Patron laughed. "I would not suggest you so casually toss away your life, boy! Bring him to me," he warned in a more venomous tone, "or you will all die, including those that are traveling with you."

Instead of cowering, Iseac was calm and resolute.

"No," he replied as he looked toward their assailant.

"Then you are a fool and will die here with them." With

those words, the former Patron raised his hand in the air and the Norians began to advance. The Golans released a volley of arrows ahead of the charging Norians, who had little plumes of dust rising behind them.

Samuel was hidden by the Ackalans, who were standing just behind Iseac. He could not see them, but could sense the arrows as they drew near. He waved a hand in the air and the arrows suddenly lost their momentum and dropped to the ground.

The charging Norians were now sixty yards from them, their weapons raised high; the sound of their pounding feet increased.

Faray's heart was racing, his palms sweaty as he prepared to meet death. He tightened his grip on the hilt of his sword. They were fifty yards away, then forty, then thirty. Just then, a gust of air shot sand in front of the Norians, blinding their view. As sand and dust filled the air, the Ackalans rushed in, and it began.

Metal rang and bones snapped, followed by the howling sounds of death as Norians fell.

Iseac had been watching in deep concentration. When he swung his hands out toward the ground, it sent all the sand and dust into the air in the direction of his wave.

Samuel could see the clear impression of those in the fog of sand and dust, and he released several volleys of arrows into the chaos. Even with their thick skin and armor, the Norians dropped to the ground like flies from the lightning bolts of Samuel's silver arrows.

Faray had joined the charge with squinted eyes inside the fog of sand. He could hear the clashing sound of weapons ringing around him as he made out the impression of the massive creature that could only be a Norian. It was almost upon him when he heard a swooshing sound. The Norian–twice his size, with arms the size of a horse's hind legs–fell straight toward him. Before he could react, it fell on him, knocking the wind out of Faray's lungs.

The massive head of the Norian rested over his shoulder with a hole in it, leaking blood, while the rest of his body was buried under the beast.

It was hard to breathe with sand and dust everywhere, but Faray made himself take slow breaths, coughing in between. With a considerable amount of effort, he managed to push himself out from under the Norian. He could still hear some fighting going on, but it was ahead of him.

What was going on, he wondered as he covered his nose with his left arm. The dust was beginning to die down when he heard the galloping sound of something approaching. He froze, watching as a brown mare galloped past him with the lifeless body of a Golan dragging along beside it.

Faray listened for anything else before continuing toward the sound of the fight. The farther along he went, the more clear the air became. When he was beyond the dust, he could see men fighting with the Norians and Golans, and it wasn't just the Ackalans.

****

The former Patron and Rogan rode into the dust storm, impressed with Iseac's futile attempt to create cover. "The Anamerian is going to die regardless," the former Patron thought as his horse moved in a trot, with Golans riding on both sides of him. The Golans had their arrows notched.

A spear suddenly appeared through the chest of one of the Golans and he dropped to the ground. The others turned to see what was behind them, and to their surprise they saw men dressed in cloaks the color of the desert running toward them. Their cloaks made it hard to focus on them, as they appeared to mingle with the sand.

"Rogan, take care of it," the former Patron said. "I will deal with the Anamerian and get the boy."

Rogan turned his horse around, taking with him some of the Golans and the Norians, and they rode off to meet the people of the desert.

****

The edge of Tremay's shortsword was stained with blood as dust settled around the body of a fallen Norian. The ground was beginning to absorb the orange pool that had begun to build around its neck when Tremay sensed something close by. He turned just as the dust in front of him suddenly parted, revealing men on horseback.

"Bollan," Tremay said to himself, recognizing the former Patron. Just as the words left his lips, several arrows were launched at him. He deflected some while evading the others as he ran toward Bollan, moving with incredible speed. His feet barely touched the ground, like a cat in full stride, before he leaped into the air, crossing his arm mid-flight. The sun reflected off the razor edge of his blade on his descent.

He was suddenly seized in the air, frozen in place and unable to move as he stared at Bollan, who looked at Tremay with the same contempt one gave to a bug, as if saying, 'Did you think you were going to get anywhere with that charade?'

He waved his hand in the air and it sent Tremay flying, far enough that no one saw where he ended up.

As if following a beacon, Bollan led the Golans toward Samuel. Iseac appeared in front of them with his quarterstaff held planted on the ground by his side as if blocking the way.

"Don't kill him," Bollan said as the Golans moved into a semicircle. They aimed for nonvital organs and fired. The arrows all dropped to the ground a few feet from Iseac as Samuel waved his hand. As the Golans reached for more arrows, they were brought down by silver ones that flew from behind Iseac. Bollan made no attempt to deflect the arrow meant for him as he watched it skid past him.

His eyes narrowed as he looked at his men that had fallen. He stepped off his horse and started walking toward Iseac, a broadsword suddenly appearing in his hand. The blade was wide with a red edge, as if pulled out of a forge fire.

Iseac spread his legs apart in a ready stance with one hand holding his quarterstaff at a fifty-degree angle, ready to pounce.

"I am going to enjoy this," Bollan thought as Iseac positioned himself for an attack. With a yard between them, they charged each other.

Bollan sent the first blow, which Iseac deflected with his quarterstaff and, on his retraction, spun his quarterstaff toward Bollan's head. Bollan shifted his head to the left, with the quarterstaff swooshed past him, the force tossing his hair.

He hadn't expected such force from someone he thought was weak. He shifted back as Iseac brought the quarterstaff to a stop with one of the tips pointed at him. He looked at Iseac; this time he would not hold back, he vowed, and he sent several deadly blows in rapid succession, which Iseac manage to evade or deflect.

Bollan moved his weapon with ease as he shifted from right to left. One of his blows came with such power that it pushed Iseac to the ground.

Iseac spun his legs in the air in a cartwheel motion, using his quarterstaff to spring back to his feet in a single motion as Bollan came to meet him. Bollan did not charge, but walked, this time, with his robe swaying as he approached.

Bollan showed no sign of exhaustion from all his effort, with the heat appearing to have no effect on him. He even seemed to grow stronger with every attack. Iseac noticed that Bollan's ring got redder as the fight continued.

Bollan's confidence grew from the power he was receiving from his ring. With each attack, he could see Iseac getting slower with exhaustion as beads of sweat ran down his face. He went in again and again, picking Iseac apart with every second or third blow: first on his chest as it ripped through his garment, then his upper thigh, and a few seconds later, another to his right arm. Unable to hold on any longer, Iseac dropped to one knee, his quarterstaff holding him up. His arm felt like lead and his chest was on fire, unable to breathe. Bollan seized Iseac with an invisible claw, raising him into the air. He pulled Iseac toward him so they were standing face to face.

"I told you your decision was foolish," he said before pushing him to the ground.

Iseac tried to stand as Bollan walked toward him, dragging his blade on the ground. Bollan had raised his hand to deliver the final blow when something zipped past Iseac. He looked up to see several silver arrows sticking out of Bollan.

Distracted by his confidence, Bollan had let his guard down, forgetting about his real target. The arrows protruded from his hands and head as his weapon slipped from his fingers and he dropped to his knees. Mustering his remaining strength, Iseac stood up.

"And I told you the same," he said, looking down at Bollan.

As death came for him, he began to laugh, a terrible, choking laugh that spewed blood. He was still on his knees with his cloak swaying on his side from the wind.

"It's all over, and no one can stop him," Bollan muttered as he drowned in his own blood. There was silence, and he dropped to the ground. As he did, Iseac lost consciousness and dropped to the ground also.

Chapter 29

Stain of Death

"Is he going to be all right?" Samuel asked as Annora stepped out of Iseac's room with two other maids.

"We'll find out soon enough."

"What do you mean?" Samuel asked.

"His condition is something I've not seen before," Annora said, not pleased that she didn't understand it herself. "He doesn't have a fever, but something is inside him that is not part of him. A strange toxin is the only way I can describe it, that only he can fight. The remedies I've given will help strengthen and heal his body. There isn't much else we can do but wait and see."

Samuel was unsure what to make of the news. He opened his mouth to ask another question, but Annora cut in. "You need to get some ointment on your burns and get some rest yourself. We'll talk more later. Right now, I need to attend to your other friend," she said, referring to Tremay, who was badly injured and should have died from being tossed wildly into the air.

"Angela," she said to one of the women by her side, "please take care of this young man and see that he gets something to eat."

****

Light flooded his eyes when he opened them and Iseac squinted until he slowly adjusted. He stared briefly at the yellow roof that was illuminated by the light dangling from it. In disbelief, he wondered how he was still alive. Groaning under his breath, Iseac turned his head and saw Elena sitting next to his bed. She smiled at him and he tried to reassure her he was okay.

While it was subtle, Iseac couldn't help noticing her nervous twitch; something about it that pricked his thought, but why did it matter, he wondered and as he was about to brush it aside, he remembered. It was the same look she had on her face when Perry, a friend of theirs, lost most of the fingers from an accident in the field, and when her cousin Chadrum's wife died in childbirth. It was the look of wanting to be brave when something bad has happened.

So what was wrong? Did he want to know? Maybe she didn't think he was going to make it.

His head felt like a reverberating bucket, even with the little attempt he made to move, but he needed her to see that he was okay. He looked at her reassuringly.

"Help me up," he said, and she did, even though every part of him ached.

"Where are we?" he asked.

"Somewhere safe," Elena replied. "Right now we are all under strict orders that you get your rest. I was allowed to stay with you under strict condition that a Council member be notified immediately when you woke up. I better go let them know."

"Wait," Iseac said. "How is Samuel?"

"He's fine and worried about you, like everyone else," she replied before closing the door behind her. He relaxed.

Stripped of his clothes except for a simple robe, he looked around the room, trying to figure out where they were, when someone opened the door. It was a woman dressed in a white gown.

"I'm Annora," she said in a voice as clear as water and soft as silk. "How do you feel?"

"I...I'm fine," Iseac stammered as he stared at her.

Annora possessed an elegance and grace that held his gaze.

She was around forty-five, which was just past her middle years, if he was to guess. Her eyes were dark brown with pure silvery gray hair. As she stepped close to him, she placed two of her fingers on his chest as if listening for something, long enough for Iseac to take two breaths.

He did not try to pull back, but looked at her.

"It is a privilege, young Anamerian, to meet you," she said.

She wasn't the first one to have made this observation. Iseac remembered his meeting with Gabram when he was twelve and he made a similar remark, but how did she... He disregarded the thought; it did not matter.

"Where are we?" he asked changing the conversation.

"You are in Olinar cave, which is to the south of Amito-Mountain."

"Amito-Mountain was several hours away from where the fighting had taken place," Iseac thought as Annora was speaking.

"You and your friends were brought here by Elwin and his men three days ago, and it was a good thing they were there to help.

"Several of the people that came with you were badly injured, but they are fine now, so there is no need to worry. We were more concerned about you."

"Three days," Iseac thought to himself. Had he been out for that long? That might explain why Elena looked at him the way she did.

The last thing he remembered was the former Patron dropping to the ground.

"We have much to talk about, but not now," Annora said as several dozen questions ran through Iseac's head. "I will send your friends in and have someone bring you something warm to eat; make your visit brief this time, if you can."

"Thank you," Iseac said. It seemed inadequate, but that was all he could think of.

She nodded once in acknowledgement of his gratitude. "Your clothes will be ready for you in the morning." She closed the door behind her.

It wasn't long before Samuel, who was smiling with relief, Mosley, and Tremay walked in.

"Elena was asked by the priestess to send us out if we kept you up too long," Samuel said.

"So, how do you feel?" Tremay asked. His arm was rolled up in a bandage that was looped around his neck for support.

"I feel better seeing all of you," Iseac replied. Flashes of the former Patron dropping to the ground ran through his mind. "What happened, and how did we end up here?"

"Annora has a special gift," Tremay said. "She sent men to watch out for a sign before the battle with Bollan."

Bollan, Iseac thought. It was the first time he made the link to one of the freed people from the marble seal, wondering how Tremay did it.

"They were asked to watch for the silver arrow that would come, and the men were instructed to protect Samuel and the people with him," Tremay said. "Once they saw the sign, they came to our aid. Taken by surprise, some of the Norians and

Golans fled when Rogan was killed by one of the priestess' men. They brought us here to Olinar so you could be helped."

It hadn't been more than ten minutes when Elena walked in carrying a tray.

"Okay, it's time to go," she said.

"I believe this is yours," Mosley said, placing Iseac's quarterstaff by his bedside.

"We'd better leave," Tremay said, saluting. Taking their cue, they each nodded, saluting in the same manner before making their way out of his room.

Iseac's initial concern for his friends had blinded him from noticing how stunningly beautiful Elena looked, with her red gown laced over her white chemise.

"This is not the time to be daydreaming of what might never be," he said to himself. "A war is coming, and time is running out for the other two." He needed to find them.

As he ate, Elena sat on the chair by his bed. They didn't say what they were really thinking, but made small talk, avoiding the more personal topics, such as their future together–if they were ever going to have one.

Outside the cave, Faray listened as Samuel told him all that had transpired after their separation. His encounter with the Agoras at the mines; finding Iseac and the Ackalan named Mosley passing through their town; his escape from Golans as he fled to Bremah after Iseac's capture; his meeting with Gabram the Patron; and his unlocking, about which he chose not to go into details.

Faray listened, impressed with his brother's resourcefulness; it was also heartbreaking knowing that his gift was also a curse. Each time he used it, it severed his ties to his family and people close to him.

His memories of them over time would slowly wash away, like a sandcastle built the day before a storm. He inevitably would be drawn to the source of his power and be removed from them all. If this was his brother's destiny, could he change it or help him accept what he was becoming? Faray knew this troubled Samuel.

While Faray had lost all hope, locked in a cage like an animal, Samuel hadn't given up on them. If there was ever a time he needed to be strong and supportive of his younger brother, this was the time.

"I've always wondered since we were kids why you were only interested in the bow," Faray said. "You never took any interest in the sword. Now I see why. Regardless of what happens, I know Mother and Father are proud of you."

"What are you going to do now?" Samuel asked, knowing there was nothing back home for them.

"Well..." and as Faray was speaking, Samuel could feel

something had changed. It wasn't anything he could see, just sense. The soft breeze that was once constant now had a soft pulsing feel mixed in. It was gradually growing, as if drawing close to him, and he turned toward the direction of the pulse just before someone appeared from within the woods.

"You are wanted inside," said a tall man with a complexion similar to Tremay's olive brown skin. Faray turned in surprise. The man had made no sound; if it wasn't for Samuel turning to face his direction, he wouldn't have known.

"Follow me," the man said, gesturing as he led the way.

Iseac and Tremay were already inside waiting when Samuel and Faray arrived at a strange entrance covered in vines. "He will have to wait here," the man said, looking at Faray. "The others are waiting for you inside."

The vines were parted by two women who stood at the entrance. A non-skilled observer would not have seen the plants move apart without the women actually touching them. These were Sekamin vines, a rare plant that would kill a man within hours of touching it, but it had no effect on women.

Samuel walked into a dome-shaped room with the floor covered in trimmed grass that looked like a green rug. Vines and bamboo trees lined the walls and the room smelled like spring with blossoming flowers. Young women in pairs stood around four entrances. They were all dressed in brown gowns, with wide hanging sleeves and white broaches pinned above their right breast.

Mats were set in a semicircle for each of them to sit. As Samuel sat looking around in amazement, the vines were parted and Annora stepped inside.

"We do not have much time, so I will only tell you what you need to know. The hand of the shadow knows you are here, and they will soon be upon us." Samuel looked at Iseac and Tremay; they seemed unperturbed. "There will be horses waiting for you when you leave, and you have to hurry. Your brother is already on his way," she said to Samuel. "Iseac should be able to help you find your way once you are outside. There will be supplies for you and your men," she told Tremay.

"I was told your men came to our aid," Iseac said. While he'd been thinking about asking how she knew they had needed help, he decided not to; it wasn't relevant at the moment, so he said instead, "Thank you for everything."

"It is our duty," she replied, "and I hope we meet again soon, since time does not favor us." She handed Iseac a parchment.

"This is for the king of Ditra-Vashine, and like every other king, he will be honored by your visit. Your amulet is the key to any of the Kingdoms. Let it be seen and you will have passage," she said.

"Could this be true?" Iseac wondered, as he always had it tucked underneath his garment.

"The one born of the scroll will soon be known by all, and he needs to be prepared," she said before they all felt the faint vibration.

"They are here,'" she said, gesturing for two of the young women to open the vines.

"We can help your men defend this place," Tremay said, the natural instinct of an Ackalan showing.

"I know," Annora replied, "but not this time. Now go!"

It was hard to argue with a woman who knew things before they happened. So Tremay bowed his head in salute as he left. Iseac did the same, following behind Tremay. Samuel wanted to ask a question, and then hesitated, but she saw it.

"Young man, is there something you would like to ask me?"

"Yes." Samuel dipped his hand in his pocket. "I need to find the owner of this ring and was wondering if you could point me in his direction."

She held out her hand without saying a word, and Samuel placed the ringed necklace in it.

As soon as the ring touched her palm, images of the baby she remembered holding at the cave entrance flooded her memory.

"The owner of the necklace is around the eastern land of Bayshia," she said. She did not ask where he found it as she placed the necklace back in Samuel's hand. Her finger brushed his and she looked him straight into his eyes.

"Do not be afraid of what you are to become."

Samuel stood there for another second before running to join the others.

When Iseac stood up and started walking, his vision suddenly went out of focus and things around him became blurry. He slowed down for a brief second, resting his hands against the cave wall as he moved. Just as Samuel approached, his vision came back. Iseac was glad no one noticed.

"We'd better keep up with her," Samuel said to Iseac as they were led by one of the women to an exit. They came out through a narrow entrance where horses were waiting for them, just as Annora said. Elena and the others were already there. As they mounted their horses, one of Annora's men stepped out into the clearing.

Tremay, who was about to mount his horse, stopped. The man held a boy by the collar of his shirt. Tremay recognized him immediately: it was the scruffy-looking boy who had wanted to join them. Jude, he remembered, was his name.

"Release him," Tremay said, and the man did. Jude straightened himself.

"This is yours, sir," he said as he held out his hand. Tremay recognized the hilt of the object; it was his shortsword.

"This weapon has served me well," Tremay said, "and I know it will do the same for you. You may keep it. Remember, it will protect you if you take care of it."

The boy looked at him, unsure of what to say. "Thank you, sir," he said as Tremay mounted his horse and they rode off into the woods.

****

When Bollan opened his eyes again, drawn from the abyss of oblivion back into his body, he discovered that he was standing in midair on a stage in a room he recognized. He was dressed in his same clothes, with bloodstains showing where arrows once protruded from his flesh. The arrows were no longer there. He peered into the dark around him and could see veiled faces with their eyes staring on him. They, like him, were some of the highest-ranking men within his Lord's sphere. He remembered taking the same oath as them.

Following their gaze, Bollan looked up to see a being sitting on a pedestal and his heart dropped. He knew who had claim on his soul as he looked into the eyes of his Lord. They blazed like hot coals on a winter's night. His master's form was different, but the eyes were the same. He had freed him from the marble seal and promised him power and immortality.

Bollan opened his mouth to speak, but nothing came out. As he stood there in terror, his master opened his hand and Bollan's ring came loose, flying off his finger. It flew through the air and came to rest in his master's palm. He looked at Bollan as he crushed the ring. Bollan puffed into dust and was gone.

"You have your promise," the man said in a haunting voice that pricked those in the room. The man wore a black cloak, with the inside covered in a red silk that covered most of his body. He had two red gems on each of his wrists, held in place by a black rod that was woven around his finger. The air seemed to still around him as he approached, and everyone in the room bowed their head.

"Destroy the boy and bring me the star of Lamtin," the man said. "Now rise." As those in the circle rose, their rings began to glow and their master was gone.

****

Interlude: The Anamerian stopped writing and placed his pen by the side of his ink jar. He waved his hand over the oil lamp and the lamp winked out. Tomorrow they would continue their journey in the snow and hopefully make their way through parts of Kadan's Gate, if it froze tonight. They should be able to cut their travel time and make it to the borders of Ditra-Vashine, where part of their army would be waiting, he hoped just before he closed his eyes.

Epilogue

An unusual ruckus was taking place along the streets of Palmer when Jayden stepped out of his room and headed down the old wooden stairs that creaked as he made his way downstairs to the once-lively room. He stepped outside the inn into the chilly night that reminded him that winter was fast approaching.

He stood there in surprise as flames from burning buildings on both sides of the street lit the night sky. The Hengan Red Inn where he was staying was only a hundred yards from one of those burning buildings.

Jayden looked around in disbelief, unaware of what he was breathing in until he started to cough from the smoke that filled the air. He placed his left arm over his face, using his cloak as a shield.

The Hengan Red Inn was one of the oldest buildings along this part of the street and the only place he was able to find a room he could afford. The rundown building was so old, Jayden knew it wouldn't take much to set the building ablaze and send it crumbling down.

He'd been happy to finally be able to spend the coming winter somewhere warm, and not in a barn or a makeshift tent. Now that was about to change. "Just when I thought that maybe I could catch a break after three years of continued hardship, this happens."

If he could complain, he would have; but there was no one to complain to, so he pulled his cloak tightly around himself and stepped away from the inn into the crowded street.

From what he could see, no one was trying to douse the fires on the burning shops or inns. Instead, the crowds were frantically rushing away from Terram, the small farm town on the outskirts of Bayshia.

All sorts were on the road. People with hand carts or mule carts, some carrying sacks, wagons of varying sizes and shapes–rushing east to seek refuge in the city.

Jayden was jostled along as he tried to find out what was going on, but the noise around him was so loud, he couldn't completely make out what the people were saying, except for a few words such as "under attack,"" monsters" and "invasion."

In the midst of the chaos, the town guards arrived. They were on horseback, making their way through the crowd, which was heading in the opposite direction. People moved out of the way, but they didn't stop.

Fixed on their destination, the guards rode without breaking stride. Just before they were completely out of sight, something was tossed into the air. It landed in the middle of the street with a bang, drawing everyone's attention close to the area including Jayden who was horrified by what he saw.

What had been tossed in the air was a guard with part of his body and horse missing. A loud howl that followed a second later seemed to mute everything, including the uproar that followed.

Shock held Jayden in place, while the crowds ran for safety. That was when he saw them: beasts that were half human cutting through the crowd like weeds, with parts flying at every wave of their massive weapons. As they made their way in his direction, a man appeared out of thin air, dressed in black and red.

His eyes were fixed on Jayden, who began to run as fast as his legs would take him, trying to get away. The faster he ran, the closer the figure seemed to get. It was like trying to run away from the sun.

"Do not run from me, child," the figure said in a voice that curled like a viper. Jayden stopped running, realizing it was of no use. Exasperated, he turned to face the figure.

"What do you want with me?" he asked, trying to hide the terror in his voice.

"Does it matter?" said the voice, which was that of a man. "My master knows you, peasant, and believes you are somehow different from the rest of these maggots." His tone did not hide his disdain for Jayden and the people being slain around him.

"You have been given a chance to prove yourself worthy in his service. If you do, your reward shall be infinite and you shall rule the earth till time itself ends. I will not tell you the alternative, but you must choose."

"If choosing this path you say involves destroying innocent lives, then no!"

"Innocent lives, you say." The man laughed hollowly. "You call crushing insects underfoot like them lives! If this is your choice, then you will die with the rest of this filth."

He stretched out his hand in front of him. The red ring on his finger flared and he began to squeeze.

Jayden dropped to his knees, struggling for air, and shook himself out of his sleep.

He was breathing hard as he sat bare-chested on the edge of his bed. It was only a dream, he thought. Or was it?

He placed his right hand on his neck just to make sure.

"It was only a dream," he muttered, reassuring himself. He reached out subconsciously to touch something underneath his shirt, but it wasn't there; realizing it, he looked out the only window in his room. It was still dark outside. He pulled on his gloves to cover his hands before putting on his shirt and boots. He walked out of his room, down the old wooden stairs that creaked under his feet as he tried to step out quietly. The bar was empty of people as he walked past it and unlatched the front door.

Standing alone at the entrance of the inn, he looked to the right and left of the street; it was quit. He looked up into the heavens; one of the stars seemed to flash a little brighter. He again looked at both ends of the street before going back inside, closing the door behind him. Tomorrow he would need to move again.